"Your love a**with film is over."**

In the dimness of the projection room Seton Chambers was pitiless. "You're not a genius. If you're ever going to use that talent you're so vain about, you'll have to stop pretending you know it all."

"Thank you for the lesson," Madge said sullenly.

He dismissed the sarcasm with a shrug. "My intention is not to humiliate you. You've got something, Copleigh—I wouldn't have asked you to work with me if you didn't. But right now it isn't much. And if you're going to be working in a difficult country, using huge amounts of Studio Seven's money, you're going to learn to make every shot count. And I'll be there to see that you do!"

These books may be available at your local bookseller.

For a list of all titles currently available,
send your name and address to:

Harlequin Reader Service
P.O. Box 52040, Phoenix, AZ 85072-2040
Canadian address: P.O. Box 2800, Postal Station A,
5170 Yonge St., Willowdale, Ont. M2N 5T5

MADELEINE KER

working relationship

Harlequin Books

TORONTO • NEW YORK • LONDON
AMSTERDAM • PARIS • SYDNEY • HAMBURG
STOCKHOLM • ATHENS • TOKYO • MILAN

Harlequin Presents first edition November 1984
ISBN 0-373-10739-0

Original hardcover edition published in 1984
by Mills & Boon Limited

CHAPTER ONE

JUST once more, she panted to herself. Come on, Madge, you can do it! But her legs were beginning to shake, and the school playing-field seemed enormous. She had already run round it nine times, over four miles, and she was painfully tired. *Come on,* she commanded her wobbly limbs fiercely. You're going to need every ounce of fitness up there in the mountains. And the more you train now, the easier it'll be then. She flogged herself around the floodlit field one last time, feeling as though her heart would burst, and was rewarded by a sense of achievement as she walked back to her car, her hands on her aching sides. Not bad. She was improving slowly.

In Tibet she was going to need every scrap of strength she could muster. The altitude, she knew, could leave even a healthy Westerner gasping and nauseous after a gentle hundred-yard walk. The Embassy had insisted that they be one hundred per cent fit before leaving for Tibet. Madge mopped her face dry on a towel, and zipped herself into the warmth of her track-suit. Driving home, her arms felt almost too tired to turn the wheel and shift the gears, but the glow of achievement remained. Over where he lived in East London, she knew that Charlie Molesworth would be training as hard as she. They were a good team, she and Charlie. A rising force at Studio Seven. One of their documentaries had even won a third prize at Cannes last year.

The television camera had taken her to some far-flung places—but Tibet was something outside her experience, a country shrouded in mystery and remoteness. She felt again the thrill of excitement deep inside. Tibet . . .

She knew at least a dozen other television people who would have given their eye-teeth for the chance to make this film. Scheduled to take up almost two hours of screen time, it was an important part of Studio Seven's major new series, directed by Seton Chambers, and called simply *Asia*, due to begin in the spring of next year. Already, with only about half of the film in the can, people were beginning to call *Asia* a landmark in television history, one of the most prestigious productions ever undertaken for the small screen.

Strangely, this was the first time she had worked directly under Seton. Strangely because he'd been the main reason for Madge's application to join Studio Seven some eighteen months ago. She had left film college with top marks, and there had been job offers from several studios.

But there had been no real doubt in her mind that she wanted to work for Studio Seven. In those eighteen months, of course, she had had time to revise her over-enthusiastic feelings about Seton considerably!

Despite the fact of her almost violent personal dislike for Seton, Madge had felt that to be asked to work for one of his productions, no matter how remotely, was one of the biggest compliments she and Charlie had ever been paid.

Of course, she thought modestly, she and Charlie *were* among the most adventurous young film-makers at Studio Seven, and among the most promising!

The underground parking-garage was deserted and eerie, as usual, and her skin was beginning to feel slightly clammy as she let herself into the flat.

Aromatic smells from the kitchen told her that Melissa had the dinner well under way. Mmmm! Except that she was going to have to be ruthless about her calorie intake over the next week. She didn't want to be carrying any extra weight on the slopes of Kanchenjunga.

Not that Margot Laura Copleigh, twenty-four this September, and rising rapidly in the world of television production, was carrying a great deal of extra weight right now. As she pirouetted luxuriously under a hot shower, she might have been a schoolgirl relaxing after a hockey game. Her cap of coppery hair framed a heart-shaped face whose glinting green eyes and full, stubborn mouth expressed a lively intelligence. She had the very creamy skin that sometimes goes with red hair, and her body was deceptively slender. She might even have been thought fragile; but in reality she was as resilient as taut silk—and as indestructible. No one watching the grace of her movements and the delicate lines of her neat breasts and slim hips would have guessed that Madge Copleigh had tumbled down more mountainsides, dodged more landslips, and forded more rivers than the average twenty-four-year-old was likely to see in a lifetime.

She towelled herself dry, feeling the ache going out of her thighs and stomach muscles. She was so *small*, that was the trouble. If only she'd been one of those big-boned girls with broad shoulders and big, strong hips! That was one of the reasons why she and Charlie were such a close team. Charlie, at six foot three and built to match, could afford to carry a third of her equipment in addition to his own when they were out in the field. In return, she gave her quickness and inventiveness to his solid dependability, transforming it into the highly successful combination that had got them so far up the slippery television ladder this past year and a half.

The partnership system was an important part of the way Studio Seven worked; almost all the films produced in the studio were made by well-established teams of two or three people—film-makers who had worked together for a long time, and who had become a smooth, efficient unit—people who knew each other's talents with uncanny accuracy.

Not that there had ever been the slightest hint of anything more than friendship between them, of course. Charlie was happily married, and she—well, if she were ever going to fall in love, it wasn't going to be with anyone from the television business.

'I don't know why you do it to yourself,' Melissa remarked, ladling out *coq au vin* as Madge slipped into her dining-room chair, still towelling her hair dry. 'There has to be more to life than making movies.'

'Not for me there isn't,' Madge smiled. 'And no bread, please.'

'But it's delicious! I've just baked it.' Melissa's brown eyes flashed reprovingly. 'You're not *dieting*, are you?'

'Just trying to sweat off a little avoirdupois.' She watched Melissa's reaction with amusement. With an alluring, rounded figure, and a well-developed taste for the good things in life, Melissa Bailey's vocabulary didn't include words like diet or abstinence. She always said them as though they were in italics. Madge, on the other hand, had never found self-discipline difficult. But then, despite a background that many would have called extremely glamorous, she hadn't led the pampered life that Melissa, the daughter of rich, middle-class people, had enjoyed since birth.

'Lhasa's over 12,000 feet high,' Madge said. 'The highest city in the world. The rest of Tibet ranges from much higher to a little lower—and there isn't too much oxygen in the air up there. It's going to be pretty gruelling unless we're fit enough to deal with the oxygen starvation.'

Melissa shuddered delicately at the word 'starvation', and swallowed a succulent mouthful. 'There just has to be more to life than work,' she repeated. And added, significantly, 'George Arnold's taking me to the opera tonight.' Madge simply nodded. Melissa had been hoping to snare one of her several boyfriends (she preferred the trendy businessman class, who bored Madge stiff) ever since Madge had known her. As for Madge herself, there had been no shortage of men eager to take her out, lured by her petite beauty, and a certain aloofness in her manner. There had been even more since she'd started work at Studio Seven. Unlike Melissa, though, marriage didn't appeal to Madge in the slightest. In fact, she'd managed to discourage almost all her admirers by her refusal—even her inability—to commit herself emotionally or sexually with any of them. They simply didn't move her that much; and Madge's experience of family life hadn't exactly made her eager for emotional entanglements with anyone. She and Melissa had been flatmates for two years, and had never in all that time had a serious argument—despite Madge's sometimes uncertain temper! Melissa sighed. 'It's unhealthy to work as hard as you do, Madge. Don't you ever feel the urge for a little corruption?'

'Not often,' Madge admitted calmly. 'I happen to be superb at my job. Why shouldn't I enjoy it?'

'Your modesty becomes you,' Melissa said drily.

Madge grinned, revealing enviably beautiful teeth. 'Okay. Correction—we're superb. Charlie and me. I admit that neither of us would be all that brilliant without the other. But together we're going to be one of the best teams at the Studio one day. And to stay at the top you have to keep working at your act.'

'So you keep telling me,' Melissa nodded. 'Some more potatoes?'

'I really shouldn't——' Madge said reluctantly.

'Oh, come on.' A large potato settled on to her plate. 'You're going to need your strength up there with the yaks. Suppose you meet the Abominable Snowman?'

'Then Charlie and I will scoop an exclusive,' she

smiled, tucking in with relish. 'Seriously, though, being asked to take part in this *Asia* series is one of the biggest things that's ever happened to us. It means a lot for both our careers, and we just can't afford to mess it up.'

'I bet you're thrilled to pieces about working for that *gorgeous* man,' Melissa sighed enviously.

Madge looked up with a dry smile. 'You think Seton's attractive?'

'Of course. Don't you?'

'No,' Madge said firmly, 'I do *not* think he's attractive.' Meeting Melissa's sceptical eye, she went on, 'He's an incredibly cold person—almost frigid. That's what makes him so brilliant at his job, I suppose. He's as cold and analytical as a camera or a tape-machine. Inhuman, really.' Madge pushed her polished plate away with an appreciative sigh. 'That was delicious, Melly.'

'Well, well,' Melissa said thoughtfully. 'To see him doing one of those programmes about lions or crocodiles or whatever, you'd think he really loved his subject.'

'I suppose he does—in a cold sort of way.' She thought of the unforgiving blue eyes, the craggy, impassive face she had often seen at work, and curled her lip in distaste. 'If he ever smiled, I think his face would crack.'

'He's beautiful,' Melissa said, raising her eyebrows at Madge's words. 'You've been peering down a camera lens too long, my girl!'

'He must be almost forty,' Madge scoffed. 'And he looks as though his face has been carbed out of granite—with a blunt chisel!'

'Exactly,' Melissa said dreamily. 'That's what I said—he's beautiful. And that body—he looks as though he could just sweep you up over his shoulder and carry you away . . .'

Madge shook her head at Melissa's dreamy expression.

'He'd be more likely to take the skin off your back with six words. We must be thinking of different people.'

'I doubt it,' said Melly, rousing herself with a sigh. 'You're just too young to appreciate him. Everyone else seems to think he's divine—he's not exactly short of female company, you know. He always seems to have some admiring female in tow.'

'I know,' Madge said grimly. 'I call it immoral.'

'Well,' Mellisa decided, rising, 'I'll leave you with the washing-up. I have to get ready for George. But if you happen to meet Seton Chambers some time, give him a big kiss from me.'

'I'd sooner kiss a grizzly bear,' Madge retorted, and shrugged to herself as Melly sauntered towards her bedroom. 'Men are right,' she muttered. 'Women are incomprehensible sometimes.'

But Melissa just smiled. Madge leaned forward on her tired arms, thinking.

Seton Chambers held a very special place among the people in Madge's life. He had influenced her more— and shocked her more—than any other person she could think of. She would certainly never, *never* think of him in romantic or sentimental terms. Yet her feelings about Seton were crazily mixed. In one sense, he would always be one of her idols, a man she revered as an artist, and the man whose work had been directly responsible for her own burning desire to make films.

In another, Seton would always symbolise the ruthless face of the television business to Madge. She had never forgotten the way her idealistic dreams about him had shattered against the uncompromising hardness of the reality!

Seton Chambers was something of a legend. In his twenties he had been one of the most courageous and talented photo-journalists of his time, regularly bringing in dramatic, often shocking documentaries and news clips from the trouble spots of the world. It had been a time when the whole world had seemed to be ablaze with wars and rebellions, and Seton's unflinching camera lens had recorded it all—the horror, the tragedy, the pathos.

Then, abruptly, he had turned to nature. The more cynical of his colleagues said that Seton was always one jump ahead of the game, and had foreseen that the seemingly endless wars in Asia and Africa were dying down, making way for a renewed interest in films about the beautiful things in life. He was as cold as that, they said.

Anyway, Madge had seen his famous film about the whales of the North Pacific, and had been devastated. She had been seventeen at the time—an impressionable age—and her life had been dark with unhappiness and cynicism then. That wonderful, terrible film, with its dazzling photography and haunting text, that had been the single most important factor in her decision to become a film-maker.

It had also, in a very direct way, transformed her outlook for ever. It had given her direction. Because even while the tears were still wet on her cheeks, there had been no doubt in her mind that *this* was what she wanted to do. To make films like this, films that moved and thrilled, films that left an indelible impression on the mind. Films that somehow captured the beauty in the world, and made you forget about the sorrow.

She knew, of course, that Seton's film had impressed her so profoundly partly because her life had seem so barren at the time, so empty. After her parents' divorce, and her own miserable, abortive elopement with Andrew Everett, she had badly needed to replace the sterility of her own world with something more valuable. And perhaps that need had been answered by the somehow more real, more beautiful world of the camera's eye. Yet there was more to it than that. Through Seton, she had found her vocation, the thing she did best of all, her purpose in life.

Which was odd. Even now, the irony made her smile; because the film world had ripped her life apart so many times, and those two most egocentric and shallow of film people, her own parents, had left her emotions shattered with such dreadful regularity that Madge had sworn for as long as she could remember that whatever career she chose, it would have not the slightest connection with cameras, studios, or the silver screen!

Charlie Molesworth admired Seton Chambers even more than Madge did. To Charlie, Seton would always be 'The Chief', a master whose word was law. That was the trouble with Charlie, she thought wryly; he was too easily overawed.

'Can I borrow your grey scarf?' asked Melissa, poking her head round the door. 'It'll go perfectly with my gown.'

'Of course. It's in my cupboard.'

'You're a love. Got any plans for tonight?'

'Mmm. I'm going to read those library books I got on Tibet and the Lamas.'

'Your debauchery will never cease!' Melissa rummaged through Madge's cupboard. 'What are you looking so pensive about? The Lamas of Tibet?'

'In a way,' Madge smiled. 'I was just thinking about Seton, as a matter of fact. He inspired me to take up movie photography in the first place. That film about the whales.'

'Oh, yes, I remember that.'

'Most people do.' Madge watched idly as Melissa looped the scarf elegantly around her neck. Melly had style, that was certain. The scarf, a present from her father, had never looked nearly as chic around her own neck. 'He was one of the founders of Studio Seven.'

'Who, Seton Chambers?'

'Mmm. He and Northcote Jameson and Paula Stephens and one or two others. They're still directors, most of them. I've always heard that Seton used the money he made with *The Whale's Song* to buy the studio buildings.'

'I'm listening,' said Melissa, unceremoniously hoisting her skirts to pull stockings on to her much-admired legs.

'I suppose it sounds disloyal to say I dislike Seton, but I do. I can't help it. I had a bad case of hero-worship after I saw *The Whale's Song*, which lasted right up until I left film school.' She thought back with an inner smile to the scruffy, earnest student she had been, so bursting with ideas and ideals. 'I didn't actually meet Seton until I joined Studio Seven, though. One day I bumped into him in the corridor. I sort of introduced myself, and then tried to tell him how important his film had been to me.'

Melissa looked up at Madge curiously.

'What did he say?'

'He just shrugged, and said, "So?"' A touch of bitterness tugged Madge's mouth. 'Then he walked into his office and closed the door. That was my introduction to the great Seton Chambers.' She could still remember the total shock, the feeling of having had a stone wall slammed in her face. It hadn't been so much a case of her idol turning out to have feet of clay—as his turning out to have a mask of bronze.

Melissa looked thoughtful for a minute, then stooped to slip slender-heeled shoes on. 'Maybe he was just in a bad mood.'

'No, that's his normal mood.' Madge smiled thinly. 'When he's in a bad mood, his secretaries cry all day long.'

'He wouldn't ever be in a bad mood if *I* were his secretary,' Melissa grinned. 'I'd keep him sweet.' She smoothed her dress. 'How do I look?'

'Ravishing,' Madge said admiringly, and it was true. There was a strong contrast between the two girls; where Melissa was a peony, full-blown and sensual, Madge Copleigh was a rosebud, self-contained, beautiful—and perhaps rather thorny to approach.

Melissa sighed. 'I'm only ravishing when I'm all dolled up. First thing in the morning—well, you know what I look like! But you—you've got *real* looks. Bones, and all that.'

'Bones, and not much else,' Madge smiled.

'Nonsense! You're all healthy and slim and sexy. And you look terrific in jeans, which I never do. George says,' Melissa added gloomily, 'that looking good in jeans is the real test of a woman's sex appeal.'

'Which sounds like exactly the stupid sort of thing men say,' Madge retorted.

'Oh, I've seen the way my boy-friends ogle you,' Melissa said darkly. The doorbell chimed, sending her scuttling back into the bedroom. 'Damn! That'll be George—and he hates me to be late. Be a love, and go and hold the fort for me?'

'Of course,' Madge said obligingly, and went to hold the fort.

The next morning something unusual in the extreme took place in Madge's life. Her mother came in to see her at her office on the twelfth floor of the Studio Seven building in London.

Olivia Copleigh was, in her late forties, still an actress who attracted male attention wherever she went. And Olivia Copleigh needed male attention the way other people needed food. Madge had never known anyone else so capable of generating instant publicity, making herself the centre of a whirl of solicitous activity. She had been doing it all her life, in hotel lobbies, at glittering first nights, in shops, restaurants, everywhere. She never simply walked in *anywhere*. She always made an entrance.

Which was why, even though she knew exactly where Madge's office was, she had summoned Tommy Baskerville, the handsome young Studio Seven press secretary, and one of his publicity secretaries, to escort her to her daughter. Though an escort of one press secretary and an attendant publicity secretary was admittedly almost startlingly modest by Olivia Copleigh's standards. The publicity secretary, a raven-haired beauty with clever eyes, was obviously already writing the press release in her mental notebook. And, like all the other men who met Olivia Copleigh, Tommy Baskerville was fawning.

'If you'd told us you were coming, Mrs Copleigh,' he was saying, his voice oozing charm, 'we'd have had a *proper* reception laid on for you.' He gave Madge a perfunctory smile as she rose to meet them with an inner sigh, and then turned back to Olivia. 'What can I get you? Tea? Coffee? A drink?'

'Perhaps just a cup of tea,' said Olivia, her famous smile lingering on the man's dog-like expression.

'Don't worry, Tommy,' Madge interrupted gently. 'I'll make my mother some tea right here.' Tommy's disappointment was barely disguised. Surely, Madge thought with a touch of cynicism, he had scarcely been born when Olivia Copleigh made her first film? But she was far too wise to be bothered by the way other men treated her mother any more.

'In which case,' Tommy smiled fulsomely, 'I wonder whether you'd mind just a *tiny* little reception after you've seen your daughter? Just a few photographs, and perhaps the *briefest* interview—I know the press would be so interested in your visit, Mrs Copleigh——'

'But of course,' the film star beamed. 'Fleet Street and I are old friends.' Which was, Madge thought amusedly, the understatement of the year!

Tommy and his raven-haired genie ushered themselves out. By the glint in his eye, Madge knew he'd have two dozen photographers and reporters—and if he was clever enough, heaps of flowers—waiting in preparation for Olivia Copleigh's exit. Tiny reception, indeed! Tommy's razor instinct for public relations had contributed in no small way to Studio Seven's prominence in the public consciousness.

Her mother presented a smooth cheek to be kissed, and Madge obliged, trying to tell herself the pang she felt inside was really love for this beautiful, careless creature who happened by some quirk of fate to be her mother.

'Darling.' She patted Madge's cheek in response, her wide green eyes, so like Madge's, crinkling in a mask of affection. 'Am I disturbing you?'

'You know you never disturb me,' she smiled. If there was any strain in the smile, Olivia Copleigh didn't notice. 'Sit down, Mum, and I'll make some tea.'

Olivia adjusted her primrose-yellow skirt carefully. There could hardly have been a greater contrast between her own silken elegance and Madge's jeans and blouse, her usual plain workwear.

'Have you lost some weight?' she asked, eyeing Madge's neat bottom. 'You don't look as though you're looking after yourself properly.'

'I've been on a diet,' Madge smiled. 'I don't want to be overweight for this trip to Tibet.'

'You're too thin. And you should be keeping your strength up. I can't *think* why you don't make more of yourself, Margot. You've got the looks, if only you'd do a bit more to bring them out. I'm sure no one would even *imagine* that you were my daughter.' Madge smiled again, too used to this line of attack even to reply. Her mother, whose idea of making her face was a two-hour session in front of three mirrors with a hundred pounds' worth of French cosmetics, had never been very impressed by Madge's preference for natural-looking red lipsticks and soft eyeshadows.

Nor had Olivia Copleigh ever understood her daughter's choice of simple, modern, preferably natural-fibre clothes for work. Perfume, on the other hand, was a weakness of Madge's, and one which inclined her to some of her few extravagances.

Her mother glanced disapprovingly at the bottles of instant coffee and the half-empty bag of stale crisps on Madge's untidy desk. 'You eat like a bird. Which reminds me—I've booked a table at Fabio's for lunch. Can you make it?'

'Of course.' She winced inwardly. Olivia managed to make any restaurant a temple where she was the only deity worshipped, and Fabio's was her special shrine. Come on, Madge, she told herself, she is your mother. She passed the teacup over. 'But I do have to watch my weight, or I'll be too fat to climb Kanchenjunga. You look beautiful, as always. How's Dad?'

'Late with the money, as usual.' Which meant, Madge supposed wryly, that her father, divorced from her mother after a stormy sixteen-year Hollywood-style marriage, and now back in his native California, wasn't actually at death's door. A touch of malice lit up her mother's eyes. 'I suppose he's spending every cent he's got on that German bitch. Have you *heard* about his affair with Nadia Schreier? Why, the little tart's not much older than you are——'

'Mum,' Madge pleaded gently, 'I don't want to hear about Dad's affairs.'

'But I think you *should* know what a bastard your father is——'

'I love you both, Mum.' Which was, Madge supposed tiredly, why they had always managed to hurt her so much. 'And you can't pretend that you don't have lots of men friends.'

'Not twenty years younger than me!' she snapped.

'I'm leaving for Tibet next week,' Madge ventured,

trying to steer her mother away from the topic. 'We're getting really excited.'

'Next week?' Her mother tried to look interested. 'As soon as that?' She glanced at Charlie's empty desk. 'Where's your partner with the extraordinary name?'

'Doreen phoned in this morning to say he wasn't coming to work.'

'Oh?' Her mother's eyebrows rose. 'He's not getting sick on the eve of your expedition, is he?'

'God forbid!' Madge thrust the horrible thought away. 'No, he's just a bit under the weather, so he's resting. We don't want to take any chances with this film, Mum—Tibet's only been open to foreigners for a few years, and we're one of the very first camera teams to have been given permission to film in Lhasa.' With her glinting, coppery hair and bright eyes, Madge positively radiated enthusiasm. 'Besides, it's a great honour to be asked to contribute to a series directed by Seton Chambers.'

'Ah—your hero! Of course, we in the *art* side of film-making don't have much to do with you *realism* people.' Olivia had always been overtly disparaging about the documentaries Madge made. 'But Seton Chambers is something special, I admit. Tibet, though. I mean, how interesting can it be? It's so *remote*.'

'Which is exactly why we're going to film it,' Madge grinned. 'To show people what it's like. *Asia* is going to be one of the most important television series ever shown. It really might help to bridge the gap between East and West. After all, we know so little about Asia—and it's so incredibly rich, so diverse, so teeming with different people and different cultures——' She drew a deep breath. 'And Seton Chambers has given us such a wonderful script to work from—Kanchenjunga, Lhasa, the Jokhang ... *Asia* will be watched by millions of people, Mum. And Charlie and I will have contributed. It's a real thrill!'

'You're so young,' her mother mused. 'I hope you're going to be all right, Margot.'

'I'm twenty-four this year,' Madge said defensively. 'And I also happen to be the other half of an up-and-coming film team.' She paused, wondering whether to ask. 'I don't suppose you remembered to watch BBC2 last Monday? Our film about the Farne Islands?'

'Monday, Monday,' Olivia Copleigh mused. 'Now what was I doing on Monday—ah, yes. No, sweetie, I'm afraid I didn't manage to see your film. Basil Welcome and some friends came round for drinks, and I simply *hate* inflicting the television on my guests.'

'It was only half an hour long,' said Madge, unable to keep the sharp hurt out of her voice. That had been one of their most successful films, gentle and tinged with autumn melancholy. She had so wanted her mother to watch it.

But she never did. Madge actually doubted whether her mother had ever sat through a single one of her daughter's films. The thought had occurred to her that her mother was actually afraid of doing so—afraid of discovering that her daughter's talent might be more real than her own. The thought rose up again, prompted by the disappointment of having been rejected yet again, but she thrust it away.

'It doesn't matter, Mum. It'll be on again.'

Oblivious to Madge's disappointment, her mother smiled brightly. 'Well, I can't waste all day chatting, sweetie. I only dropped by in the line of duty, and I must get on with my shopping. Will you meet me at Fabio's at around one?'

'Fine. I'll walk you out.' Taking her mother's arm as they went down the corridor together, Madge went on, 'I've just been doing some research into the Potala—the Palace of the Dalai Lama in Lhasa. It sounds a fantastic place, really quite overpowering—a city on the roof of the world. They call it the abode of the gods.

We were very privileged to be given permission to film there——'

She broke off as they approached the lift. A tall man in a dark grey suit was waiting there, one hand thrust into his pocket. He turned a tanned, rather forbidding face to glance at the two women without interest, his eyes, an extraordinarily dark blue, flicking over them dismissively. As his eyes met Madge's, giving her that jolt she could never quite shake off, he nodded curtly.

Then he turned back to his contemplation of the glowing floor numbers that foretold the lift's arrival.

He hadn't even given Olivia Copleigh the almost obligatory second glance that was the least she expected from men! Absolutely typical of Seton Chambers' rudeness, Madge thought angrily. I've been working here for eighteen months now, I'm just about to set off for Tibet to make a film for his series, and he still hasn't even got the courtesy to say good morning!

There was a heavy silence on the way down. Being ignored by a man in a lift was an experience Olivia Copleigh evidently hadn't had for almost forty years. For once in her life completely silenced by a massive snub, she merely gaped at the broad back.

Madge, for her part, maintained a seething silence. Being close to Seton always upset her badly; he possessed a kind of nerve-tingling presence which always set her hackles up. He was disturbing, and that was undeniable. She glanced at the familiar, famous face, noting the streaks of grey that had appeared in the thick, almost-black hair. There were unforgiving lines incised at the corners of those electric blue eyes, and around that downward-slanting mouth. I wonder if he ever does smile, she thought to herself. Looking at that bronzed, fiercely male face, she doubted it.

It was a relief when the lift-doors opened, and Seton strode off with little more than a curt nod to Madge and her mother.

'Pig,' Madge muttered to her mother as they walked to the exit. 'He's always like that.'

'*Very* insulting,' she agreed angrily. 'I felt like saying something. Still,' she mused, her face looking softer, 'he's fabulously attractive. He has an extraordinary sort of *atmosphere* around him. He could easily have made a magnificent actor. People with that quality have to defend themselves from the world, you know, Margot. I have to do it myself.' Madge glanced up in disbelief. Her mother defend herself from attention? That would be the day! 'All famous people build up that sort of reserve—you shouldn't be too critical.'

'Don't tell me you're also a Seton Chambers fan,' Madge smiled. 'I thought that making documentaries was distinctly down-market from your neck of the woods?'

'Seton Chambers is different. He didn't seem to have very much to say to you, did he? I thought you were so crazy about him?'

'Crazy about his work,' Madge corrected firmly. 'As for the man himself——' Words failed her, and she leaned forward to kiss her mother goodbye. 'See you at the restaurant, around one,' she smiled. 'And buy me something nice?'

'Aren't you going to walk me to the Rolls?' Olivia asked in surprise. Madge shook her head. She had glimpsed the photographers waiting in the foyer. And the huge bank of flowers. Tommy Baskerville had been clever; her mother responded very well to flowers. But Madge wasn't going to go through one of her mother's press interviews again. She'd done it too many times in her life. Tommy was going to be furious that she hadn't turned up, but let him be. He didn't have to go through life with parents like Olivia and Tyrone Copleigh.

She watched her mother walk down into the welcome of exploding flashbulbs, and shook her head slowly. Olivia Copleigh was a phenomenon. She was so elegant, so beautiful, so easy to be proud of—if only there had been any real maternal feeling under that glamorous façade. I love you, Mum, she thought sadly. But I don't think I'll ever know just what you feel towards me . . .

She caught sight of Tommy Baskerville emerging from the throng, his good-looking face creased with worry. The raven-haired genie was close behind, her clever eyes searching the crowd. Madge knew exactly who they were looking for. Herself. Her mother was amply capable of carrying off a news conference on her own—but in order to get the full publicity mileage out of the event for Studio Seven, Madge herself would have to be there.

'Not on your life,' she muttered, and slipped quickly into an empty cutting-room across the corridor. There, among the silent machines and bins full of cut film, she waited for a good twenty minutes while the hubbub died down. When she poked her head round the door, the foyer was empty. Even the banks of flowers had been spirited away by Tommy Baskerville's minions. Smiling, she took the lift up to the twelfth floor.

Dennis Quinton was waiting for her in her office when she got back, the big camera slung over his shoulder showing that he was just off on a filming assignment.

'You look busy,' she commented.

'I need some footage of otters playing for that documentary about Canada. London Zoo will provide.'

'That's cheating,' she grinned. Dennis was ten years more experienced than she, and at least fifteen years older, but she got on well with him. It had been Dennis who had interviewed her when she had first applied for this job eighteen months ago. Then she had been an eager, inexperienced photographer, fresh out of college and burning to work in the studio which counted Seton Chambers as one of its directors. How delighted she had been when he had told her the job was hers! Dennis had taken a fatherly interest in her progress ever since, and never tired of predicting that she would go far.

'Otters were thin on the ground while we were up in the Yukon,' he shrugged. 'The public won't notice the difference if I'm careful.' He scratched his thick beard with a glint in his eye. 'That's show business. Speaking of which, I hear your revered mother's in the building?'

'She's been holding a conference in the foyer right now. I opted out.' Dennis and Charlie were among the few people in Madge's life who knew that Olivia Copleigh was her mother—and among the very few who had any idea how unhappy and neglected her childhood and family life had been like.

'Did she upset you?'

'Not more than usual,' Madge smiled wryly. Dennis looked into her eyes carefully, saw the hurt there, and decided to change the subject.

'Listen, Madge, I probably won't see you again before you and Charlie leave for this jaunt to Lhasa. I came to wish you luck—and to ask if there was any help I could give you, any last-minute advice or equipment you wanted to borrow?'

'I appreciate the offer, Dennis,' she said fondly, 'but it's all pretty much under control. Charlie's off with a touch of hay fever today, but that's nothing. We leave on Friday, and we're all set.'

'Excited?'

'Electrified would be a better word,' she admitted. 'It's only a three-week tour, but we've got a tight schedule. Our Leader,' she said with a touch of sarcasm, 'has handed out his usual brilliant shooting-script.'

'Seton? You sound a bit disillusioned with him,' Dennis said.

'I just get fed up with his curtness,' Madge sighed. 'He never says hello to me, even though I'm off to risk life and limb to get the film he wants. He just nods, like some kind of superior being. It makes me sick!'

'Seton's a camera genius, Madge,' Dennis said gently. 'Don't forget that he was filming wars when you were still in your rompers.' His smile took the sting out of the reproof. 'Maybe he just doesn't notice that he's being—well, a bit brusque. But he's no machine, and he can be very kind.'

'Hah! He should have been called Satan.'

'When I interviewed you for this job,' he said, 'you told me that your admiration for Seton Chambers was one of the main reasons you wanted to work here. Things seem to have changed, young Miss Copleigh.'

'That was before I actually met him,' she retorted. 'I now know better.'

'What, just because he was once a little short with you? You must be the only woman in the building whom he hasn't succeeded in ensnaring,' Dennis judged, his round, bearded face mischievous. 'According to the typing pool, he's Studio Seven's matinee idol.'

'They've all got men on the brain in the typing pool,' Madge snorted. 'I suppose he enjoys being the focus of female attention. I'm surprised his wife doesn't go crazy!'

'Didn't you know?' He looked at her curiously, shifting his camera. 'Seton's a widower.'

'You're joking!'

'I'm not. His wife died five years ago—a car crash. I'm surprised you didn't know that.'

'I haven't made it my business to probe Seton's background,' Madge said defensively, suddenly feeling uncomfortable, as though she'd made some grave *faux pas*. As a seventeen-year-old, she'd read that Seton was married. She could remember quite clearly her juvenile disappointment at the news! Now, though, it was oddly shocking to hear that this unknown woman had been dead for years. Madge had never paid much attention to office gossip—as a camerawoman, she was out of the building more often than in it. Also, since that brush with Seton over a year ago, she had tended to avoid discussing him. Curiosity made her frown. 'Who was she?'

'Lana Chambers? She was a model. Very pretty girl, tall and willowy. I met her several times—she was full of life, a real swinger. It was hard to believe it when she was killed.'

'Was Seton—did Seton find it hard to take?'

'Husbands usually do,' Dennis Quinton said drily, sliding off Charlie's desk. 'Don't they?' He shook Madge's hand in a hairy paw, and kissed her firmly on the cheek. 'Good luck, kiddo, and pass my best wishes on to Charlie. I know this trip's going to be the making of both your careers.'

'Thanks, Dennis,' she said absently, her mind still on what he had told her about Seton. 'See you next month.' She leaned against her office door, watching Dennis's burly figure disappear down the corridor. Her eyes were thoughtful. It was hard to imagine Seton in any human relationship. Oh, she had heard the stories about his conquests—who hadn't? He was always appearing in public with beautiful and glamorous women, and Madge had assumed that he simply used them and discarded them. Rather as her father tended to do. But marriage?

She drew her fingers through the rich red mop of her hair, and pulled it back into a diminutive pigtail. The careless action revealed the slender grace of her neck and the alert, almost defiant tilt of her head, and would have proved to someone watching that Margot Copleigh had inherited more than a little of her mother's famous beauty. She secured the little bob with a clip, and sat down to go over Seton's script for the twentieth time.

The telephone on her desk shrilled, and she scooped it up automatically. It was Doreen Molesworth, Charlie's wife. For some unaccountable reason, Madge felt her heart sink.

'He didn't want to admit that he was sick,' Doreen was saying, sounding slightly tearful. 'He pretended it was just hay fever, or a cold. Oh, Madge, he's *so* disappointed!'

'What's the matter with him?' she asked, dreading the answer.

'The doctor says he's got yellow jaundice. He's had it for nearly a week.'

Madge's insides twisted. 'Oh, *no!*'

'He has to stay in bed for a month at least.'

'How awful,' Madge groaned. 'Is he feeling rotten?'

'He's been vomiting all day. He looks *terrible*—his eyes are all yellow, and he's a terrible colour. But the worst of it is that he won't be able to go on this trip to Asia now——'

'I know,' Madge said numbly.

'The doctor says there's no chance he'll be working again for three months. He's absolutely miserable about it.'

'I'll come up to see him this afternoon,' Madge promised. Her mind was still spinning with the news.

It was the end of the expedition, of course. For both of them.

'You will be able to find someone else, won't you?' Doreen asked anxiously.

'I don't think so,' said Madge, her own voice flat with shock and disappointment. 'Now not.'

'Oh, Madge——'

'Seton will pull us off the job and send another film crew. That's his usual response when something like this happens.'

'Oh, Madge. I'm so sorry for you . . .'

'You've got enough to worry about,' Madge said, struggling to inject a smile into her voice. 'It honestly doesn't matter. There'll be plenty more assignments like this one. Give my love to Charlie—and I'll see you both later on.'

She replaced the receiver numbly.

There was a queer, sick feeling inside her. There wasn't a hope that Seton would let her go with a new partner—this film was too important to risk with an untried team.

Madge knew of old what it felt like when dreams crumbled. You just couldn't believe it at first. And then you cried. She'd been so excited to be given this job, so eager to get out to a strange land. And now it was all over.

CHAPTER TWO

MADGE dropped her briefcase, unopened, beside her desk, and slumped into her chair. A great deal of her sparkle had evaporated since yesterday. Nor had the commiserations helped, though there had been plenty. Even her mother, in between gushing at Fabio's and being gushed over in return, had found time to say that she was sorry. Charlie and Doreen had actually comforted her at Charlie's bedside (it was so typical of Charlie to care more about her disappointment than his own).

Now, though, she felt so flat, so colourless. She hadn't even bothered to come to work on time this morning, and she was always early in to the office. Charlie's empty desk stared at her mournfully.

She picked the phone up listlessly when it rang.

'Yes?'

'So you finally decided to turn up. I've been ringing you since nine-thirty.'

The deep voice jolted her upright with a guilty start. Then her latent antagonism rose up.

'Who's calling, please?' she asked frigidly—even though that vibrant voice was familiar to half the nation.

Seton Chambers ignored utterly her attempt to irritate him.

'My office, Copleigh. Ten minutes.' The line clicked dead in her ear, and she stuck her tongue out furiously at the receiver before replacing it. She could just tolerate being called 'Copleigh'—he called everyone by their last names—but she absolutely *hated* his brusqueness right now. It grated on her raw nerves.

She sighed again, her eyes feeling heavy with tears of

frustration. This interview would be to tell her he was
giving the Tibet film to someone else. Damn, damn,
damn.

Oh, Charlie, she groaned, did you have to get
wretched jaundice, of all things? And the last thing she
felt like right now was facing Seton.

Come on, Madge, she grimaced, getting up. Why
be afraid of him? He can only scar you mentally for
life.

Seton Chambers' office was functional, uncluttered,
and brightly lit by a huge window which let in a
fabulous view of London. The only thing that saved the
office from being stark was the immense photograph
that covered one wall. It was a still from *The Whale's
Song*, one of the most haunting images of all—the
majestic sweep of a whale's tail-fins etched against a
North Pacific sunset. That was how the film had ended,
Madge knew, with that poignant question—are the
whales doomed to extinction? Typical of his vanity, she
thought, to have this picture dominating his office. But
the impression was almost magically powerful, and she
had to tear her eyes away from the photograph to give
her attention to what Carla Dickens, Seton's personal
secretary, was saying. Seton, leaning back impassively
in his chair, was staring out of the window with those
strangely deep blue eyes, apparently indifferent.

'Normally,' Carla was saying in her cool voice, 'you'd
be offered the chance of working with another partner.
With production at such a crucial stage, though, that's
not advisable in this situation.'

'I see,' Madge said dully, vaguely wondering whether
the beautiful Carla, with her soft mouth and cool grey
eyes, was another of Seton Chambers' past conquests.
What was she doing here, anyway? Seton should be
telling her all this himself.

'The series director can't risk the possibility that
things might go wrong between you and your new

partner, spoiling the film,' Carla went on. 'Nor can we waste any time in trying you out with different partners. You're due to leave in five days—and there are vital deadlines to be met.'

'Sure,' said Madge, not even bothering to keep the boredom out of her voice. Did he really have to tell her all this through his secretary? She shot him a resentful glance—but Seton, seemingly utterly unmoved, clasped his big hands behind his neck, and continued to stare out at the view of London. He just didn't care. This was the biggest disappointment she had ever faced, and he just didn't care. 'So you're going to ask another team to make the film? I understand.' Madge shrugged painfully. 'Is that all?'

'That's not all,' Seton said. She looked up in surprise at the sound of his voice. 'You're not being taken off the job, Copleigh. You'll be working with me instead.'

'With you?' she blinked. 'I don't understand.'

'Seton's going to take Charlie Molesworth's place,' Carla explained. She tapped her pencil on to the pad in her lap, watching Madge with not unfriendly eyes.

'Seton?' She gaped from Carla to Seton Chambers' craggy impassivity.

'You don't like the suggestion?' Seton asked calmly.

'Do I have any choice?' she asked drily, still getting over her surprise. Her heart was beginning to pound uncomfortably. Work with Seton Chambers? That might be worse than not going at all!

'Of course you have a choice, Copleigh,' he said, his hard eyes expressionless. 'That's what Carla's been trying to explain. If you've got any objections, let's hear them.'

Objections? She tried to marshal her dazed thoughts. Apart from her instinctive antagonism to Seton, she knew that this was a chance in a lifetime. Seton almost never worked with others—he was a loner, a one-man outfit. To be able to work next to Seton, maybe pick up some of the genius he had in such abundance ... That might just be a valuable experience in terms of her career—even though she knew exactly what he had in mind. Which would be using Madge as a general run-around. 'But you're the series director,' she said slowly.

'That doesn't stop me from making a personal contribution to the series,' he replied. The deep sapphire eyes were steady on her face, the rough-hewn features expressionless. 'I'm a photo-journalist first and last, Copleigh. I may have entered the exalted realms of direction and production over the past few years, but I still prefer to make my own films. I had intended to make the Japanese section of the series anyway, in the autumn. But the Tibetan section is too important to leave to chance. It's a unique opportunity in television history.' He paused. 'So—now I'll be making that section as well. I've allocated my other work elsewhere.'

His arrogance brought the blood to her cheeks.

'*You'll* be making the Tibet section?' she repeated bitterly. 'And what'll I be doing? Carrying your valise?'

'I didn't mean that.' He fielded her angry glare indifferently. 'Naturally, I'd expect you to be working with me all the way.'

'How generous,' she said scathingly. God, he was infuriating! She just could imagine how much she'd be allowed to contribute to the film now. Exactly nothing. Because her presence would be strictly for appearances. So—he was just going to walk in, was he, and make her his obedient little helper?

Carla Dickens, obviously perturbed by Madge's high colour and angrily sparkling eyes, interposed gently.

'It'll be a unique chance for you, Madge.'

'But *I* was scheduled to make this picture,' she said, aware of sounding childishly petulant, and not caring.

'Correction,' Seton said. 'You and your partner were scheduled to make this picture. And I did the scheduling.' His eyes, such an intense, unyielding blue, made her drop her own gaze. 'Come on, Copleigh,' he said, his voice dropping into the husky purr that had melted a million hearts during his documentaries, 'I'm not going to cut you out of your share in this film. Why react like this?'

'Because you're just taking the whole film away from me,' she snapped. She didn't believe his smooth reassurances for one minute. He *must* know how much she disliked him; why didn't he either do the job himself, or ask her to work with someone else? But the lure of Tibet had hooked her, and she knew it. 'You asked me to make this picture in the first place——'

'I asked you and Molesworth,' he interrupted. 'Molesworth has now chosen to get jaundice—which leaves you without a partner. And without a film.' He leaned back in his chair, his broad shoulders straining at his suit with a hint of raw muscle under the Savile Row silk. 'If you aren't interested, of course, I'll assign you elsewhere, and make the Tibet section on my own.'

'I don't see why you didn't do that in the first place,' she said rudely. 'Why involve me in your plans at all, now that my partner's out?'

'Seton didn't want to interfere with your contract,' Carla said quietly. 'You signed a contract to do this film, and you can't be taken off unless you agree to be taken off.'

'My contract? Is *that* what this is all about?' She looked at Seton with angry scorn. 'You needn't have gone to all these elaborate lengths, Mr Chambers. You should have just kicked me off the project—isn't that your usual way?'

'This is not to do with your contract,' he said quietly. 'It's to do with a film. You can't make it on your own. I'm offering you the chance of working with me. For the last time—are you interested?'

Madge gritted her teeth. Her temper, as always, had boiled over at an inopportune time. Unattractive as the deal sounded, there was still a chance for her to get to Tibet—and to pick up a lot of experience on the way. Right now, if she was wise, she had to stay cool.

'I'm interested,' she said tightly.

'Then you agree?' His voice was velvety.

She struggled with herself again, aware of how petulant and uncooperative she must be seeming. 'It doesn't look as though I have any alternative,' she said. She could sense Carla Dickens' inward sigh of relief. And Seton smiled. His face didn't, as Madge had so often predicted, crack. But it certainly wasn't a smile that shed much warmth. It added one or two new lines to the weatherbeaten masculinity of his face; and it might have conveyed anything, from cynical amusement to a dry contempt.

'No sensible alternative,' he agreed. His voice shifted from that famous purr into his usual uncompromising authority. 'That's settled, then.' That voice, Madge realised sourly, was a perfectly-controlled weapon that Seton used to get whatever he wanted. In this case, while it hadn't exactly melted the marrow in her bones, his velvet growl, so caressingly intimate, had contributed largely to her capitulation. Maybe she had seriously underestimated Seton Chambers' ability to charm. Her mother had been right: he would have made a fabulous actor—for villain's roles. Anyway, she sighed to herself, half a loaf's better than none.

'I'll get straight on to the Embassy,' said Carla, rising, 'and ask them if they'll transfer Charlie's visa to you.' Seton nodded, and with a quick smile at Madge, Carla swished out, leaving a faint trace of expensive scent.

Something that had been puzzling Madge for the past few minutes suddenly became clear.

'That's why you had her in here,' she said accusingly. He raised an eyebrow at her.

'What?'

'Carla—your secretary. You made her do all your talking for you—so that I wouldn't make a scene!'

'I usually find that Carla exercises a restraining influence,' he acknowledged calmly. 'Especially when there's a chance that female susceptibilities are going to be outraged.'

She glared at him with eyes like angry emeralds. 'You mean when you're going to hoodwink some unsuspecting woman, you get Carla Dickens to hand out the poisoned chalice—to distract attention from yourself?' She shook her head wryly, uncertain whether to be angry or amused or both. 'That's completely Machiavellian!'

'An interesting description of my tactics,' he said, considering her with midnight-blue eyes. 'And not inappropriate. Running a big television studio does bear certain similarities to ruling a mediaeval princedom. There are the same intrigues, the same plots and back-stabbings and complicated situations. The same call for delicate handling.'

'It sounds right up your street,' she commented sweetly, and his bronzed face broke into that Cheshire-cat smile again.

'Working with you may not turn out to be so dull after all, Copleigh.'

'I'm glad to hear it.' His easy assurance niggled at her, keeping her resentment just under flash-point. There were so many things about this man that upset her, disturbed her, infuriated her. And people just gave in to him all the time—no one ever had the guts or the brains to resist him. Why *should* he get away with it all the time? She covered the obstinate set of her mouth with a saccharine simper. 'I just hope you'll be able to keep up, Mr Chambers.'

'Oh?' His eyes dropped to an appraisal of her slim, taut figure. 'You're a ball of fire, right?'

'Oh no,' she said, her slim eyebrows rising

delicately over eyes that brimmed with innocence. 'Just young.'

He didn't react, much to her annoyance. And also to her relief. This man had been so important in her life for so long; she had crept round him, worshipping from afar—why *should* she stay afraid of him for ever? He was only a man—and suddenly she wanted very badly to get through to him, and sting that male arrogance just a little!

'I understand your desire to get back to the groundwork of making films, Mr Chambers,' she pursued. 'Lots of men at your age want to recapture the—er—vigour of their youth.'

'Really?' he purred, tilting his head sideways, as though truly interested by what she was saying.

'Oh yes,' she nodded, still wide-eyed. 'It's a well-known syndrome of middle age.'

'Well, well!'

Inwardly gleeful, Madge kept an ingenuous smile in place. 'It's just that a lot of Tibet's over twelve thousand feet high. And the altitude can play havoc with people who—well, who aren't in the peak of condition.'

'Indeed?' The expression in those level eyes hadn't changed by so much as a fraction. That golden-tanned skin, she thought, must be as impenetrable as a rhinoceros's! 'I take it you're in peak condition, Copleigh?'

'Well,' she said smugly, 'I've been training. I run four miles every evening.' She glanced at Seton's expensive cream shirt-front, and was disappointed to see that instead of the pot-belly she had expected, his stomach seemed flat and hard. 'I swim every weekend. And I've been on a strict high-protein diet.'

'You've been a busy little bee,' he commented, showing not the slightest sign of being impressed by her catalogue. 'Where do you run?'

'Round St Bernard's school playing-field.'

'What time?'

'From six, or thereabouts,' she said, beginning to feel slightly uneasy. 'Why?'

'Oh,' he said, rising to his full six feet, 'because tonight I'm going to join you.'

'You are?' she blinked.

'Indeed. I have a rather tiresome dinner-party to give at nine—but Carla and the caterers will handle it between them. There'll be plenty of time for a quick run first. After all, I'd better make sure I'm fit, as you say. I don't want to hold you up when we're in Tibet.' For the first time, Madge began to have the feeling that she might have been rather less than clever in trying to insult Seton Chambers. It wasn't that there was any kind of threat in that rocky face. She just had the feeling that he was amusing himself letting her run on. The way a tomcat amuses itself with a doomed mouse.

She rose, her saccharine smile now uncertain.

'Ah, that will be nice.'

'I thought you'd approve.' With his hands in his pockets, he looked down at her calmly. 'Goodbye, Copleigh.'

The sensation of having made a silly mistake was deepening ominously as she walked out. God in heaven, what had got into her? As she thought back to the things she had said, her heart quailed. She could have lost her job back there. Maybe she just had. Post-tension weakness made her knees unsteady for a few seconds. She was going to have to keep her tongue in check if she didn't want to find herself suddenly out of work!

Thank heaven he hadn't been really annoyed by her stupidity. Why had she done it? Because he wasn't Mr Nice? Simply because he got under her skin?

That's unprofessional, she told herself angrily. Don't forget what Dennis said—Seton was filming wars when you were still in pigtails. Even if you hate the man, you have to respect him. And if you're going to be working with him over the next few weeks, you're going to have to keep your feelings under control, Copleigh. And think of it as an honour. An unwanted honour, but an honour nonetheless.

It was incredibly hard to know how to treat a man like Seton. Trying to anger him by making out that he was a geriatric cripple, she realised, probably wasn't the ideal way. He hadn't even bothered to reply to her taunts, but she had the feeling that if he had, she'd now be a smoking ruin. What was best? A cool indifference, probably.

Her solemn mood gave way to a spurt of joy as she entered her office. She was going to Tibet after all! Not with poor Charlie—but she was going, at least.

She did a quick pirouette into her chair, her good humour bubbling up again. She was going to make that film! Not even Seton was going to spoil her pleasure in that. She might even learn something from him. And tonight she was going to run his legs off. She'd wipe that Cheshire-cat smile off his lips!

A sharp stab of pity for Charlie made her reach for the telephone. Telling Charlie that she, at least, was still going to Tibet might help to console him in his gloom. *I wish it was you, Charlie,* she thought as she dialled the number, *I wish it was you . . .*

The afternoon passed a lot more happily than yesterday. Charlie had been touchingly glad that she was going to Tibet after all, and had seemed thrilled that she was to work with his revered 'Chief'. Her mother, whom she had called just afterwards, seemed to think that she had been given a huge compliment. She didn't bother to disillusion her, but she was franker with Melissa as she hauled on her track-suit at five to six, feeling a butterfly of nerves at her forthcoming encounter with her new partner.

'What he needs is someone to carry his bags and tip the porters,' she said. 'I don't pretend that it'll be anything like teamwork. Yours truly will just be the general dogsbody.'

'Isn't that a bit unfair to him?' Melly asked.

'You don't know Seton,' she said darkly, tying her track-shoes. 'But talent practically drips from his fingertips. Maybe something'll rub off.'

'I'd let Seton Chambers rub *anything* off on me,' Melly said enviously, watching Madge run to the door. 'Be good . . .'

She was at the field by six sharp, a trim figure in her grey track-suit, and was jogging impatiently on the spot by the time Seton's Porsche pulled up at the gate five minutes later. She surveyed the sleek, ultra-modern lines of his car with a jaundiced eye. It was a very expensive and highly-geared two-seater. A selfish man's car. Being a director of Studio Seven must be profitable. Seton swung out in a track-suit top and shorts, and locked the door.

'Am I late?'

'Five minutes.' Madge surveyed the broad shoulders, and dropped her eyes to his legs. They were long and lean and muscular. And their golden tan suggested no shortage of outdoor exercise. The sensation of having made a bad mistake returned in full force, but she shrugged the feeling off. He turned, his startlingly direct gaze catching her eyes on him.

'Shall we go?' he commanded. She nodded, and set off beside him, the cool evening air pleasant on her warm cheeks.

It didn't take her more than ten seconds to realise exactly what she was in for. He moved with the rangy grace of a hunting leopard beside her, his powerful body swinging easily as those long legs fell into the unmistakable rhythm of the experienced long-distance runner. Her heart sank right into the soles of her

Korean track-shoes. Oh, *hell*. Middle-aged? Seton Chambers was a powerful man at the very height of his powers.

And tonight, Copleigh my girl, he's going to run you into the ground.

She dropped behind him, utterly miserable with herself. This wasn't the first time her cheek had landed her in bad trouble—but she was going to remember this occasion very well indeed. Dully, she watched his legs. They were as sleekly efficient as the Porsche he drove— or, Madge guessed bitterly, any of the other possessions he would choose. He ran from the hard power of his hips, the long muscles pulsing with easy grace, hypnotic, relentless . . .

The circuits spun together in a relentless blur. After ten times round the field, she was soaked in sweat, and an agonising stitch had settled itself viciously under her ribs. Seton had set a faster, smoother pace than she was used to, and she had long ago passed the point at which she usually stopped. The long legs in front of her were barely beginning to gleam with sweat, and he seemed to have just settled into his rhythm. Sweat stung her eyes, blurring her vision. God, she hurt! Her breath was ragged in her throat, and her lungs were on fire.

Eleven times round, and her legs felt like overcooked spaghetti. He glanced over his shoulder at her, noting that she had fallen a good ten yards behind. Madge gritted her teeth fiercely. All right, you bastard, she swore, if that's what you want! She flogged a few desperate ounces of strength out of her aching muscles, and caught up with Seton, the effort making her giddy. *I'm not going to give in*, she vowed. I'll drop in my tracks first, I swear it. I swear it. But I won't give in . . .

The twelfth circuit was sheer purgatory, though, and Madge's will was straining to snapping point. They had run five miles in just under an hour, and she had stretched her body's resources to their limit. Her legs had begun to wobble alarmingly, and when she staggered for a moment, it was touch and go whether she just crumpled on to the grass like a pole-axed steer. Then, miraculously, strong hands took her shoulders, guiding her off the circuit and steadying her as she staggered to a halt beside their cars.

She didn't look at him, just dug her fists into her burning sides, and slumped forward from the waist, sucking the sweet evening air into her lungs. When at last she looked up, her face wet and scarlet with exertion, his eyes held no triumph. Their deep blue depths were as calm as they had been that afternoon in his office. The only concession his iron-hard body had made to the run was a film of sweat that made his skin gleam like burnished gold, and set glittering highlights on the crisp hair at the base of his muscular throat.

'Okay,' she panted, feeling weak, 'I asked for this. Why not run me into the ground? You know you could do it.'

'Because I didn't intend to humiliate you, Copleigh.'

'What was this, then?' She wiped sweat from her cheeks, reflecting that she had probably never looked less alluring in her life.

'Just an object lesson.' The strange, fathomless smile crossed his face again. His mouth, she noticed with the clarity of exhaustion, contradicted the hard authority of his eyes with a hint of restrained passion. 'Also a way of finding out if you were really fit enough for this trip.'

The irony of it made her grimace. 'Do I make the grade?'

'You've got a long way to go,' he said calmly. 'You'll probably be okay.'

'Oh,' she said, feeling distinctly crushed. There was no warmth in his face or voice, not the slightest touch of concern for her heaving sides and shaky legs. He's a machine, she thought, a machine that amuses itself by outdoing humans.

He reached out and felt the dampness of her track-suit. 'You'd better get into a hot bath,' he commanded, 'or you'll get a fever.'

'Yes, *sir*,' she said with tired irony. She ran slender fingers through her wet hair. Perspiration had darkened it to a deep Indian red, and damp curls clung to the delicate lines of her cheeks and brow. Oh, for a luxurious bath, and then bed! 'What are you going to do?' she asked, somehow feeling she ought to say something, though she would sooner have been flayed alive than apologise for her rudeness that afternoon. Seton lifted one eyebrow.

'Me? Run, of course. I haven't extended myself yet. I had you to think of.' She glared at him quickly, but he didn't seem to be mocking her. 'If I'm to sit round a table all night with an assorted gaggle of politicians and film stars, I might as well take my frustrations out now. Think you can drive?'

'Of course,' she snapped, her boneless arms belying her confidence. He nodded, his eyes taking in the whole of her petite figure in one glance, and then trotted back to the circuit without further farewells. She watched him, shaking her head numbly. In a few seconds he had regained that hunting stride, his body moving into overdrive with effortless grace.

'Damn you,' she whispered, knowing she would never say those words to his face. Tearing her eyes away from him, she walked slowly to her car. God, she felt as though she'd been through a mangle! She climbed stiffly behind the wheel and buckled her seat-belt. Her green eyes flicked up to watch Seton through her windscreen. He moved so smoothly, so fluently. What a magnificent body he had to go with that razor-edged mind! Small wonder that women found him so irresistible. He was magnificent, unique. And totally ruthless. What sort of lover, she asked herself idly, would that add up to? Were there any reserves of tenderness beneath that godlike façade? Would the gold melt in lovemaking, or would he be totally hard, dominant, unyielding?

Come on, she told herself drily, don't be a damned fool, girl. Don't start kidding yourself that Seton Chambers is human. And speculating about someone else's love-life is just plain indecent. Again, though, she had to consciously tear her eyes away from him in order to check behind her as she reversed out of the drive. Her calf-muscles were almost too uneven to handle the interplay of accelerator and clutch.

She drove slowly through the suburban streets, feeling that she was a lot sadder and wiser than five hours ago.

Okay, round one to Seton. And if you've got any brains, Copleigh, just call that game, set and match.

Her office phone began ringing the minute she walked in the next morning. A night's sleep had stiffened her into near-immobility, and she felt as though she were creaking as she lifted the receiver.

'Madge Copleigh.'

'My office. Now.' The line clicked dead. She shut her eyes and uttered a quick prayer for strength. If Lhasa was going to be anything like this, she'd consider giving up photography altogether! Three minutes later she was in Seton's office, once again confronting those penetrating eyes.

'Olivia Copleigh is your mother,' he said, not inviting her to sit down.

She nodded.

'You saw me with her the other day.'

He shrugged. 'I don't remember.' You wouldn't, she thought sourly. 'But she was certainly here. I've just had a memo from Tommy Baskerville informing me of the great event.' So Tommy Baskerville had made a formal complaint about her defection! The spiteful little creep! Madge said nothing, wondering what lay behind that golden mask. 'It was an ideal publicity occasion,' he went on. 'Glamorous film-star comes to visit her whizz-kid daughter at Studio Seven. Life from both sides of the camera. Banks of flowers, ten cameramen, six reporters.' He paused, his eyes implacable. 'The only thing missing was the whizz-kid daughter.'

'I don't like press conferences,' Madge said tightly.

'No one likes press conferences,' he growled. 'They're a fact of life, like disease. What makes you so special that you don't have to attend them?'

'I just didn't want to.' His eyes took in the obstinate set of her mouth and the defiant tilt of her chin, and then dropped to a ruthless appraisal of her figure. She had abandoned jeans today in favour of a summery skirt that clung to the graceful lines of her figure, and was high enough to show off her trim legs. But as his eyes raked over her body, Madge was certain he was no more inwardly moved than if he had been studying a machine that for some unexplained reason wasn't working properly.

'Listen, Copleigh. This is a comparatively young, comparatively untried studio. We may be successful right now; but that success could evaporate next week. All we have to recommend ourselves is our abundance of talented brats. Like you.' The arctic expression in his eyes made her wince involuntarily. 'We need all the publicity we can get—everything. Personally, I don't give a damn about politicians and film stars and all the rest. But I put up with them. I give dinner-parties for them. I shake their hands for minutes on end, and show my teeth to the cameras while I'm doing it. I and the other directors employ a staff of overpaid nancy-boys to lay on big receptions for them.'

The hard mouth was grim. 'Are you getting the message, Copleigh? The television business exists on publicity. It floats on a river of publicity. It eats publicity, drinks publicity, sweats publicity out of its pores.' He stabbed an aggressive forefinger at her chest. 'And *you*, young lady, God help us all, are part of the television business. This television business. Understand?' Feeling as though she had been hit on the head with a half-brick, Madge could only nod at him wide-eyed. 'Okay. The next time your mother arrives at the studio, you damn well co-operate with the publicity department. First and last warning.' Madge watched him, her stunned feeling giving way to fury as he leaned back in his executive chair, thrusting his hands into his pockets so that the hard muscles of his stomach came into relief under the silk shirt he wore.

'Is that all?' she said shakily, her hands clenched into fists.

'No,' he grated, 'that's not all. I've reserved one of the projection-rooms downstairs. We're going to have a quick lesson in film technique this morning.'

'I'm afraid I've got other things arranged,' she gritted, her heart-shaped face white with anger and humiliation. How *dared* he talk to her like that? What did he think she was, a spoiled child?

'Other things are cancelled from this moment.' He rose in one fluid stretch, and scooped a thick file off his desk. 'Come.'

Madge had to bite back the swear-words on the tip of her tongue, her whole body rigid with anger. He pulled the door open, and paused. One eyebrow arched dangerously. 'Well?'

'Mr Chambers,' she said in a quiet voice, 'if we're going to work together——'

'If we're going to work together,' he interrupted brusquely, 'we're going to have to get used to each other. We've got exactly four days. Now, shall we cut the cackle?' He swung the door wide, and strode off down the corridor. Speechless, Madge followed. And they called this man charming?

The small projection-room he led her into was

deserted. Inside the luxurious auditorium was a console which automatically controlled the projection equipment behind the ten rows of plush seats. She sat down stiffly in the middle of the third row, still too angry to even wonder why he had summoned her here.

The lights dimmed to near-complete darkness as Seton punched buttons on the console, and then the small screen flickered into life. As the numbers counted down on the leader, he sat down beside her. She flinched as his hard shoulder bumped her in the dark, his proximity, as always, setting twenty alarm bells ringing all over her body. Right now, she felt as though she really hated him, as though his very touch would raise her creamy skin in weals. Then her attention leaped to the screen. The camera was panning slowly across a dusty African landscape, the heat making the scene of dry grass and derelict-looking thorn trees shimmer. Slowly, the title faded in. She didn't have to read it. *People of the Namib*, a film she and Charlie had made twelve months ago. One of their best. It had been bought by BBC 2 as well as by two Independent Television companies, and had done well in the U.S.A. since then. She glanced quickly at Seton's profile beside her, then turned back at the film. What was this all about?

'Right,' said Seton, leaning forward. 'I want you to watch the photography from here on. Especially this bit about the women pounding millet.' Madge obeyed, the memory of making the film rising sharp in her mind. She could almost smell the dust in her nostrils, feel the heat . . . 'See the way that clip cut away to the children? Much too fast. I'd never have done that. You should have let the camera run for a good minute more. You've established a good shot, nice light, nice mood. Why waste it? This stuff,' he said contemptuously, gesturing to the shots of children playing, 'is useless. Dime a dozen stuff.'

She sat in silence, her anger seething, as he ran the film on to a section further on, the tribal dancing.

'This section should have been the highlight of the film. It's got everything—colour, excitement, atmosphere. Except that the camera's wobbling around like a leaf in a gale. Guaranteed to give the viewer instant seasickness.'

'Those new Hafflers are heavy,' Madge retorted resentfully.

'Exactly,' he said drily. 'Which is why people use tripods.' He pointed scornfully to a shot in which the camera was indeed wavering distractingly. 'Why spoil it for the sake of a one-minute adjustment? Next time, when you're setting up an important piece like that, use your head, Copleigh. Use a tripod.'

Again she said nothing as he wound the film on further. But she was stinging inside as though he'd cut her skin with a whip. No one had ever said such hurtful, cruel things about her work!

'This is one for the book,' he said, the scorn in his voice rasping. 'Watch the focus in this section. Notice anything?' She didn't reply, her anger curling up like a spring inside her. 'That's right,' he nodded. 'It's non-existent. Looks as though it was shot through the bottom of a milk-bottle.' He reached out to the console, and the film slowed down to a quarter-speed. 'Observe the focusing at this point, Copleigh.' She watched, her mouth set in a tight line, as the camera focused on a group of people weaving, went out of focus, came back again, went out again . . .

The fact that it really was a dismal performance didn't lessen her sullen anger any the less. He didn't have the right to humiliate her like this, as though she were a novice in her first year at film school! 'You had five goes at focusing on those people,' he said quietly. 'Why subject the viewer to your ineptness? When in doubt, girl, focus the lens *before* you start shooting.

That way the viewer doesn't have to wait for you to get it right.' He glanced up at the shot, which was still ever so slightly out of focus. '*If* you ever get it right.'

He spun the film forward to the next section. And the next. And the next. Madge's initial resentment and pain dulled into a deep, sick feeling in her stomach. He was utterly merciless, exposing weaknesses, probing faults in technique, never missing an error or a place where the picture could have been improved.

The crazy thing was that each time, he managed to hit on a section that she herself had done. Charlie's contributions to the film went undiscussed. He either had an unerring instinct for camerawork that was almost miraculous, or he had asked one of the film editors to tell him which sections had come from Madge's cameras.

He couldn't know her work that well; he must have asked. She ground her teeth. Absolutely typical of his meanness, his unfairness, his love of proving himself superior to others!

And not a single facet of her technique went unanalysed. Every little bug, every sloppy habit or careless moment, every mistake or omission, was systematically shot down. She felt like a patient on the operating table. Without the benefit of an anaesthetic. So that she was aware of each cut the scalpel made. If only Charlie had been here beside her, to help her field the criticism—but he wasn't.

Being ill in bed with jaundice, she thought at one point, was probably heaven compared to this systematic destruction.

The film flickered into blackness, and Madge's shoulders sagged with relief and defeat.

He switched on the lights, rose without looking at her, and pulled off his jacket, slinging it over the seat in front of him.

Pale-faced, she watched the broad power of his

shoulders, the tapering suppleness of his waist, and wondered vaguely whether he'd ever been a boxer. He'd have a devastating punch.

'I'm saying this again, Copleigh.' He turned to her, those dark blue eyes watching her seriously from under the heavy brow. 'My intention is not to humiliate you, merely to teach.' She looked down at her hands, which had twisted themselves into a knot in her lap, and thought, who are you trying to kid, Chambers? I know exactly what your intention was. You really enjoyed that.

'Thank you for the lesson,' she said, not even trying to hide the bitterness in her voice. She was startled when a strong hand cupped her chin, and raised her face so that her green eyes stared into his. 'Okay,' he growled, 'so you're a whizz-kid, a super-brat. You've got talent, and a lot of well-meaning people have told you you're a genius. Well, your honeymoon with movie photography is over. Because I'm telling you you're not a genius.'

The painful grip on her chin relaxed, and she slumped back sullenly in her chair, her eyes furious. 'And if you're ever going to get anywhere,' he went on quietly, 'and really use that talent you're so vain about, you're going to have to start working. Not just indulging yourself, and pretending you know it all. Because you don't. No one ever stops learning in this game.'

'Yes, sir,' she said acidly.

'You and Charlie Molesworth have made a successful team so far,' he said, ignoring her feeble attempt at sarcasm. 'Want to know why? Because Molesworth is ultra-careful. A plodder. Someone who really works hard at getting everything perfect. And Molesworth's care allows you to get away with slapdash work that even an amateur would be ashamed of. He covers up for you.' He held up a big hand. 'You've got something,

Copleigh—I would'nt have asked you to work with me if you didn't. But right now, it isn't much. And if we're going to be working together on a tight schedule in a difficult country, using huge amounts of Studio Seven's limited funds, you're going to have to learn to make every shot count.' He stood up, slinging his jacket over his shoulder. 'Lesson over. And don't forget our date tonight.' She blinked at him dazedly. 'St Bernard's field, six sharp.' Her inner wail of misery must have shown, because that Cheshire-cat smile crossed his face again as he walked to the door, leaving her slumped in her seat.

At the door, he looked back, the midnight-blue eyes delving into hers with controlled power.

'That's right,' he purred, reading her thoughts. 'I'm a bastard, Copleigh. A grade-one, twenty-four carat bastard. I'll see you tonight.'

CHAPTER THREE

MADGE's crisis reached a head on the eve of their departure. It wasn't just that her dislike of Seton had deepened, and in deepening, had clouded the prospect of the trip. She also felt that he had put her under a strain that was intolerable. The six o'clock runs, oddly enough, had been among the most pleasant of their contacts. There, at least, she didn't have to talk to him, or keep up their frigid social relations. She simply ran, and after twelve circuits, which still stretched her resources, she simply dropped out, let Seton run on, and drove home muttering.

But his analysis of her work had shaken her. He had been grossly unfair; she *didn't* think herself a genius. Perhaps she had been complacent, even a little vain, but that didn't justify the way he had demolished her. He had challenged her in the most direct way possible, and she had the feeling that out in Tibet, she was going to be under the magnifying glass all the time. Required to produce her best, one hundred per cent quality, with no mistakes allowed. And that, in her book, meant persecution.

But she couldn't pretend that her dislike for him was uncomplicated. After that unforgettable interview in the projection room, she had gone to the Studio Seven archive and quietly requested Seton's last three films. She had watched them, all alone, in the same projection-room the next day, two films about animals, and a documentary about life in a Chinese peasant commune.

They'd been stunning—humbling. Next to that quality, that magic, the films she and Charlie had made

51

were fumbling things, the work of tyros. Seton's vision of the world seemed so intense, so unflinching. He saw life steadily, and saw it whole—and in his films he captured, in some mysterious way, the very mystery of existence, the essence of beauty. From his point of view, she had to admit, her own work was extremely feeble stuff. But we can't all be Seton Chambers, she thought resentfully. He expects too much!

To add to her complications, she had been becoming acutely aware of Seton as a man.

Since that unforgettable brush-off, she had been content simply to hate the image of Seton the Ruthless. Now, though, she was beginning to feel that the Great Dictator image might be exactly that—an image which he cultivated very carefully. And she had been starting to feel that something else, more human and intriguing, might lie beneath. Or was that just wishful thinking, a sentimental hope that such a dazzlingly attractive man might be nicer than he seemed? After all, she didn't have any evidence for that supposition, beyond the hopelessly vague feeling called feminine intuition. In any case, this interest in what made him tick was something new, and potentially something highly dangerous. She was becoming fascinated, despite her dislike and her mistrust, with his face, his gracefully-moving body, the person who lay behind the mask. As she drove home after their run on Friday night, Madge reflected that Seton Chambers was probably the most remote, inaccessible person she had ever met. If she had had any inkling, when she had first seen *The Whale's Song* at seventeen, of Seton Chambers' true nature, she might have changed her mind about going into the movies for ever!

He gave nothing away. Nothing. That craggy golden mask concealed every emotion as securely as a mountain conceals the precious ore in its veins. Even his eyes, a stunning hundred-fathom blue though they were, and made all the more dramatic by thick black eyelashes and heavy eyebrows, were strangely impenetrable. You didn't look into them. They looked out at you. Nor did Madge fool herself that his Cheshire-cat smile was anything more than another kind of mask—like the husky, sexy voice, or the impeccable suits he invariably wore, complete with hand-stitched Italian shoes, and (she'd noticed) a gold Rolex Oyster Perpetual. Who had given him that? Lana?

Despite herself, she was fascinated by the thought of his marriage. It was so hard to think of him in any personal relationship, really caring, really showing that he cared. It was far easier to imagine him, like her own father, as a man who enjoyed women's bodies, and simply cast them aside when they began to bore him. As a lover, she could imagine, he would be more than fulfilling. That muscular body would be devastating in bed, urgent, dominant, overwhelming——

Madge! She yanked the handbrake up with unnecessary violence as she jerked the car to a stop in the deserted garage. For God's sake, what had possessed her to let her thoughts run on like that? Seton's love-life wasn't even remotely her concern. But she found that her hands were shaking as she unclipped her seat-belt.

Purely tiredness after the run, she told herself grimly—and with a fierce effort, erased the vivid image that her mind had so shocked her with, the image of Seton's hard body against hers in bed, his mouth hungry against her own . . .

She was almost relieved to find that Melissa was out with George. In her present mood, she just wanted to be alone. She brewed strong black coffee, then stripped off her track-suit and took her coffee to drink in a deep, hot bath. Lying back in the bath, she stared down blankly at her own body. The neat, dark tips of her breasts were taut above the water, refusing to soften in the delicious heat, and somehow the keyed-up feeling was slow in going out of her flat, hard stomach and slim legs. She gulped at her coffee, trying to ignore her own body's obstinate tension.

All from one mental slip? You're losing your grip, Madge. You're no virgin, remember? Andrew Everett should have been enough to put you off sex for life. If you had any brains. You're no kid of seventeen any more, getting unfulfillable longings for the first virile man you meet. You're a calm, sane, grown woman with a good career ahead of you.

She had been barely more than a child when she and Andy had eloped. Oh, her body had been adult enough—but her emotions, twisted by the miserable years of the divorce, had been unready. As always, regret pierced her as she thought of the brief, futile relationship she and Andy Everett had had. If only she had resisted then, she might have grown up in a more ordinary way. And she might not now be so confused, so easily put off balance by someone like Seton . . .

Unbidden, the thought of those deep blue eyes rose in her mind again. Maybe he was a lot more attractive than she had been prepared to admit. Maybe she had been stupidly unaware of Seton's power to charm, his very considerable sex appeal. Again, she thought of the hardness of his body, the shocking power of his will.

'Damn!' She flung her sponge across the bathroom, and slopped water violently over her soapy shoulders. Furious, she hauled herself out of the bath in a miniature tidal-wave, and wrapped her shaking body in a towel. 'I am *not* going to start developing a fixation for that man,' she said furiously. 'You hear me? *Not!*'

She stalked through into the living-room, in a state of sharp discontent with herself, Seton, and the whole world. Maybe she should pull out right now. Not go to Tibet at all. Let Seton go on his own, without her to carry his cameras.

Maybe she should leave Studio Seven altogether—

take Charlie with her, and look for another studio. Maybe even the BBC, or freelance work. Something a thousand miles from Seton Chambers.

He was too damned attractive. Why had she never seen that before? He was always locked away in his eyrie on the fourteenth floor, a mystical personage above ordinary mortals. And now, for the first time, when she was due to be working closely with him for the next month and more, she had discovered the magnetic sex-appeal that everyone else in the world had always known about.

God, if she only had someone to talk to, a real mother or father. She glanced at the clock. She had promised to go and see Charlie and Doreen tonight to say goodbye. But it would have been so good to have spoken to someone closer, someone who might just possibly understand and advise. On impulse, she curled up next to the telephone and started dialling her father's number in California. It would be earlier in the morning there than her father liked, but what the hell. She hadn't spoken to him for six months. And he was a man—maybe he could tell her how to deal with someone like Seton . . .

The rich Californian drawl was a little slurred when, after eight rings, Tyrone Copleigh answered the telephone.

'Dad! It's me.'

'Madge?' There were grunting sounds, and she smiled as she imagined her father sitting up in bed, his aristocratic, actor's face still creased from not enough sleep and too much whisky the night before. 'It's practically dawn!' A yawn, and then the first hint of affection—stagey, but music to her ears. 'Well, hi there, gorgeous. Great to hear from you. Terrific. Are you in trouble?'

'No. I just felt like talking to you.'

'Of course, sweetheart. Any time.' Madge caught a

woman's voice in the background, sounding sleepy and irritable. There was a rasp as her father's hand covered the mouthpiece, but she still caught the rumble of his voice: 'It's only my daughter, honey. Go back to sleep.' His voice came back more clearly. 'Sorry, Madgie—just the radio. Hey, I caught that film you made, the one about London Zoo. It was on NBC last night.'

'Did you like it?'

'Loved it!' There was no doubting the enthusiasm in her father's voice, and Madge grinned with pleasure. Unlike her mother, her father was always generous in his praise of her work—and unlike her mother, prepared to admit that documentaries could be a high form of art. 'Everyone said it was terrific. I was proud of you.'

'Thanks, Dad.' Immensely cheered, she went on, 'Actually, I phoned to tell you I'm leaving for India tomorrow evening. I'm making a film about Tibet with Seton Chambers. We've managed to get special permission from the Chinese authorities to film in Lhasa.'

'That sounds great!'

'It's for part of this new series that Studio Seven's making about Asia. Seton's the series producer.'

'Great. Terrific!'

'It's a real honour to be asked to work with him, Dad. He's brilliant, dedicated. I'll learn a fantastic amount.' She hesitated. 'He's just incredibly cold and demanding.'

'Great.' This time, the rich voice was perfunctory. Madge grimaced, then turned it into a wry smile. Her father's attention-span wasn't all *that* long where his daughter's career was concerned. He didn't want to listen to her sounding off about Seton and all her little problems. 'Hold on, sweetheart.' There were more raspings, and a muffled exchange of voices. This time the woman sounded angry, and when her father came back on the line, his voice was slightly ruffled. 'Sorry, kid.'

'Sounds like that radio's giving you a lot of trouble,' she said drily. Tyrone Copleigh's famous chuckle drifted down the line.

'It's one of these flimsy modern models. Very temperamental, and difficult to switch off. That's great news about your trip to—er—wherever.' She heard the sounds of a cigarette being lit. 'Have you seen your mother lately?'

'Yes, I saw her the other day. She's fine. She was complaining that you were late with her cheque.'

'Ah. Well, I've had a spot of bother up here, Madge, and your mother can be kind of unreasonable sometimes. To put it bluntly, the old witch is quite capable of setting her lawyers on to me. Could you do me a huge favour, Madgie? Go and see your mother and try and explain things to her. She'll listen to you. Just say that your dad's a little short this month——'

'No.' Not again, she thought unhappily, not all over again.

'Come on, sweetie, just try and get her to be reasonable——'

'I'm sorry, Dad,' Madge sighed, cursing herself for her stupidity in mentioning the money, 'I'm not going to intervene between you and Mum ever again. It's your business, not mine.'

'Honey, I know you've had a tough time in the past. I won't ask you again, I swear it. Just this once—please? You were always on my side, weren't you? Didn't you once tell me you loved me more than your mother?' She winced. He'd once dragged the statement out of her, with floods of tears, at the age of fifteen. The childish words had subsequently been hurled to and fro in the court-room until they'd lost their meaning to her. 'You've got the knack of talking her round. To tell you the truth,' he said, his voice dropping expertly into

sincere confidentiality, 'I'm in between pictures right
now, and I've had a lot of expenses lately. Couldn't you
tell her that I'm in hospital—a heart attack, say——'

'*No*, Dad.' She drew a deep breath. Why did it always
have to be like this? Why couldn't they ever want her
for her own sake, love her for what she was? All her life
she had simply been a pawn in their endless games.
When she was a child, she had been a valuable publicity
asset to be displayed and exposed at every available
opportunity. Her first memories were of posing for
publicity stills with her parents, both flashing million-
dollar smiles over her shoulders. When their marriage
had soured, she became a weapon they used against
each other, trying to play her off against each other
with a callousness that even now amazed her. She'd
been a go-between when legal complications entangled
them, the subject of a very bitter and very public court
battle during the divorce. And after that, a toy to be
pampered for a week or two at a time, until boredom
set in, and then shuffled off out of sight. Boarding
school. When in America, summer camp. Friends'
houses, 'just for the night'. Days and weeks alone, or in
the company of curious strangers, who would whisper
to their guests, never quite soft enough so that Madge
couldn't hear, 'Tyrone and Olivia Copleigh's daughter.'
Until she had packed her suitcase that night, and run
and run and run . . .

'Tell her yourself, Dad. I don't have any influence with
her, anyway. She doesn't listen to me, she never has done.'

'Okay.' She knew that petulant note so well, and her
heart sank. 'If that's the way you feel, Madge.'

'I'm sorry, Daddy.'

'Don't be.' Exhaled smoke fluttered against the
mouthpiece. 'Okay, sweetie, I have to go now.'

'Already?' she said, her voice inadvertently regaining
the tremor of a lost little girl's. 'I wanted so much to
talk to you——'

'Some other time, huh?' The indifference in the stagey drawl cut like a razor.

'Okay,' she said miserably, knowing this was her punishment for not agreeing to intercede with her mother.

'So long, sweetheart. Happy trails.'

'Look after yourself, Dad.'

'Sure.'

Click. Brrrrr. Another severed connection, another silence, another empty hole in her life. She put the receiver down slowly. There wasn't any use in kicking. It had always been like this. Always would be. And until she learned to stop hoping for real responsibility from either of them, she'd just keep on getting hurt. She got dressed, and went out to see Charlie and Doreen.

Doreen Molesworth was a woman as tiny as her husband was big. But her cornflower-blue eyes were none the less observant for seeing the world from a four-foot-ten vantage point, and as Madge settled herself on the end of Charlie's bed, Doreen had noticed the tiny creases of tension between Madge's brows.

'Anything worrying you, Madge?' she asked gently. Poor Charlie, his face sallow and his eyes yellowed by jaundice, smiled.

'Of course she's worried! She's just about to set off to make the most important film of her career.'

'An hour ago,' Madge grimaced, 'I was just about ready to pack the whole thing in. I may still do it.'

'You can't be serious!' Charlie gaped.

'Never more so.'

'But why? What's the trouble?'

'Seton Chambers.' She sipped her coffee with absent eyes, remembering her explosion of feeling in the bathroom a bare hour ago, and wondering whether Charlie would ever be able to understand. Doreen glanced quickly at her husband, then at Madge.

'What is it, Madge? Don't you get on?'

'That's the understatement of the year.' She gave them a very quick résumé of her frozen relationship with Seton, and they listened in silence. 'I don't know,' she concluded lamely, 'I suppose it all sounds rather petty to you. But I honestly don't know if I can work with someone like Seton. He's so cold, so arrogant. Charlie and I always consult each other about what to do. With Seton, it's a flat order, and no alternative. Sometimes I really think he despises me.'

'Look,' said Charlie, his honest face frowning uncomfortably, 'you got off to a bad start with him, right? You implied he was too old to make the Tibet film. He showed you he wasn't. You admit yourself he didn't actually humiliate you. Then he tried to brush up your technique a little—and let's face it, partner, you aren't always the most careful camerawoman in the world. But that seems about it, to me at least. Why make such a big production out of it?'

'Because he's completely indifferent, Charlie.' She struggled to find the words, aware of how confused she felt. 'He's indifferent to me as a person. He treats me as though I were some kind of computer, without feelings or—or emotions.' She shook her coppery head, the emerald light in her eyes serious.

'I can't understand it,' said Charlie, looking at his pretty little wife. 'I admit I've never worked with the Chief personally, but he's the best there is, Madge. I can't think of a single reason why you aren't getting on.'

'I can,' Doreen said quietly.

'You mean you know why he hates me?' Madge enquired, raising her slender eyebrows. 'Don't keep me in suspense!'

'I don't think he hates you, any more than you hate him. But I've seen Seton Chambers on television lots of times—we always watch his films. And he's an extremely magnetic man. He has a kind of charisma that's hard to explain—a kind of presence. And you're a very attractive woman. Not just pretty—vivacious, clever, charming.' She smiled. 'A woman who was less sure of her husband might get very jealous at seeing someone like you going off to the jungle with her man, Madge. Now the two of you are thrown together without much choice. In a situation like that, tensions are bound to arise.'

'You don't think I'm harbouring an undiagnosed crush on Seton, do you?' Madge asked sharply.

'Is that such a strange notion?'

'If you saw the way Seton treated me, you'd think it was!' She fought down her mind's acknowledgment that what Doreen had said contained a hard kernel of truth. 'And as for him being attracted to me—not on your life, Doreen! I'm a machine to him. He probably doesn't know whether I'm male or female. I can tell,' she said irritably, looking at their thoughtful faces. 'I can tell by the way he looks at me, the way he talks to me. If he happens to bump into me, or touch me accidentally, there's not a flicker in his eyes. It's as though he were touching a piece of furniture. A woman can tell when a man's affected by her, you know that. And Seton isn't even distantly interested in me.'

'I see,' Doreen said slowly. She took Madge's cup for a refill. 'Is that a statement—or a complaint?'

Madge looked up sharply, the obstinate curve of her mouth becoming tight.

'It's a statement,' she growled. 'And the moment it becomes a complaint, I'll throw myself off the peak of Kanchenjunga. Now, can we talk about something else?'

But later, on the way home, Madge's mind echoed with Doreen's words. Of course she was affected by Seton! How stupid she'd been to deny that. She wasn't the first, nor would she be the last—he simply reached out without effort, and moved people. That was the kind of man he was. And she knew that if she didn't start acknowledging Seton's magnetism—and her own powerful susceptibility to it—she'd find herself in more trouble than she'd be able to handle.

'Know your enemy,' she whispered to herself. 'Isn't that what they say?'

Seventeen thousand feet. Night. Outside the jet-liner's windows, the majestic darkness unrolled for a thousand miles in all directions. Madge looked away from the window with an inward sigh. The flight out from Heathrow had been heavily booked, but at Istanbul, at midnight, most of the passengers had disembarked, and the plane was now three-quarters empty.

She had buried her face in a thick novel from the minute she had fastened her safety-belt, primarily to avoid having to talk to Seton, but with the ostensible excuse that air travel bored her stiff.

Now the in-flight movie was over, and all the conversations had drifted into silence. In the green glow of the cockpit, Madge guessed, the pilots would be drinking coffee, and thinking about the beds they had left behind or the beds that lay in wait. The stewardesses had all melted away to wherever they snatched some sleep and restored ravaged make-up to emerge with their smiles and complexions intact for breakfast the next morning. Seton was lying back in the seat beside her, his eyes closed, his hands resting on the book he'd been reading.

Even in sleep, Madge thought, he didn't unwind. His body seemed flexed, alert. His broad chest moved in slow, regular breaths. She laid her cheek against the Dacron of her seat, and stared at his face from under lowered lids.

Why had she ever thought him ugly? Melissa had been right: he was beautiful. Beautiful in the way any flawless male animal was beautiful. The soft reading-light on the overhead console drifted down on to the golden skin, glinting off the long lashes, pooling shadows under the fierce lines of his cheekbones. There was command in his face, an unquestioned authority. But there was more. There was a curve of sensuality at his mouth, a fullness to his lips that spoke both of arrogance and a taut passion that was held in check by a steel will.

Of course he was beautiful, she thought again. Everyone else knew that. Why hadn't she noticed until now? Had she really been too busy? Or had her very admiration for him obscured her real feelings? *The Chief*, she thought, with a touch of acid in her smile. The master, born to command. How satin-smooth his skin was, his hair thick and crisp for all it was silvered at the temples.

And she had called him old! There probably wasn't a more attractive age for a man than this, the fullness of his maturity, when power and intellect and sexuality were moving into their fullest range ... She dropped her eyes to the exquisitely-cut suit, the silk shirt that he'd tugged open at the throat, so that the top of his chest, hard and swept with dark curls, was visible. It was a strange thrill, being so very close to him, and yet so remote. At least her heart wasn't pounding in her throat, the way it usually did when he was close to her. At least there was no hostility now.

So close. She could feel the warmth of his skin, smell the sharp tang of his cologne. She could even smell on his breath a trace of the single brandy he had drunk, and which still stood, not quite finished, on the fold-down table. She could have reached out her slender fingers and touched the curve of his lip, traced the line of his chin and the column of his throat, spread her fingers slowly across the warm velvet of his deep chest. Would he waken? She could even lean across, gentle as a night breeze, and brush his lips with her own ...

'Press conferences.' His silky voice made her eyes widen into startled green pools for a second, and her heart jumped painfully. Had he been awake all the time, aware of her scrutiny?

'Wh-what?' she stammered.

'You told me you hated press conferences.' His eyes opened, almost black in the soft light, and met hers with a hard jolt. 'Why?'

She straightened in her seat, her heart still pounding, and hoped to goodness he hadn't felt her eyes on him, or read her secret thoughts.

'It's a long story,' she said uninformatively.

'It's a long flight.' The invitation was so casual as to be almost indifferent, but for some reason Madge took it up—where she mightn't have taken up a direct interrogation.

'I've just been through too many of them. Simple: my parents are both actors, Mr Chambers.'

'I know. Tyrone and Olivia Copleigh.' The Cheshire-cat smile wasn't friendly. 'And let's cut out the "Mr Chambers" stuff.'

'All right—Seton.'

'I think "Chambers" will do,' he said gently. 'For now.' He picked up his brandy glass and drank off the last gulp, staring reflectively up the aisle. 'Your parents divorced seven years ago.'

'Yes,' she said in surprise. 'How did you know?'

'I read *Jackie* and *17* every week.' He shot her a satirical glance. 'You had a hard time?'

'I've had a hard time since the day I was born,' she said drily, wondering whether any other human being would ever be able to understand. 'There was a press conference around my crib, and the flashbulbs hurt my eyes so much that I cried.'

His glance raked her face. 'And twenty years later you still opted for a career in the movies?'

'On the other side of the cameras. But maybe you're

right at that. I was probably crazy.'

'You're not doing too badly,' he said indifferently. 'You're a super-brat with a couple of prizes under your belt already. Maybe you'll even grow up to be a super-super-brat.'

'You don't like me, do you?' she asked softly. 'I get on your nerves. You only dragged me along on this trip because I'd signed the contract. But you'd as soon have me jump out of that window as come with you.'

'That's putting it much too harshly.' His smile took in her breasts, bra-less for comfort, which were making soft, revealing peaks against the cashmere of her sweater. 'You're easy on the eye.'

'Am I to take that as a compliment?' she enquired tightly, her cheeks flushing as she folded her arms over her rapidly stiffening nipples.

'Let's get back to your involvement in the movies. Okay, so you were a lonely Hollywood child who never knew real love. Your first words were "Where's Mummy?" You saw the desolation that the film business could produce in human lives. Didn't that put you off?'

'No,' she said shortly, totally uncertain whether to take his tone seriously or as another piece of mockery. 'If you really want to know, Mr Chambers——'

'I told you—just Chambers.'

'*Mr* Chambers—*you* were chiefly responsible for my going into this line of business.'

'So you once told me.'

She looked quickly up into the handsome face.

'You remember that?' she asked in disbelief.

'Sure.' His eyes met hers lazily. 'You came up to me about a year and a half ago, just after you signed up with Studio Seven, and told me that *The Whale's Song* had made you decide to take up filming.'

'I'm amazed that you remember,' she said ironically. Maybe his perception of her was a lot sharper than she had bargained for! Had he really remembered such a tiny incident from nearly eighteen months ago? 'You weren't exactly charming on that occasion,' she added.

'I don't collect hero-worshippers.' He stretched, cat-like, and glanced at her. 'So making movies is your way of compensating for a childhood deprived of love?'

'It's a lot more complicated than that,' she retorted. 'I make films because it's what I do best.'

'Is that so?' he drawled. His eyes probed her expression. 'You feel strongly about your art?'

'Don't you?' she countered. 'You ought to know how I feel.'

Unexpectedly, his face softened. 'Perhaps I do. About what you've just told me—about your parents—I'm sorry. I'm sorry you were hurt then, and I'm sorry you still get hurt now.'

'Oh, I've got over it ages ago,' she laughed in confusion, utterly taken aback by his gentleness.

'Having got over it doesn't mean it doesn't still hurt,' he said quietly. 'I can see it in your eyes. I wish you'd explained a little of this that day I bawled you out in the office.' She made a helpless gesture, still wondering whether his compassion was yet another mask. 'There's not much I can say to make it any better for you,' he went on, his eyes on hers. 'If you're in the market for advice, then mine is to tell yourself that you've got your own life now, and to remember that your childhood's behind you. And if your childhood was troubled, then you've got the best years yet to come. Not so?'

'I suppose that's true,' she mumbled, feeling suddenly embarrassed.

'After all, you're young enough to get over just about anything.' A wry, almost bitter touch gathered at the corners of his mouth. 'When you get a little older you'll find that it's not so easy to walk away from emotional disasters intact.'

She glanced at him quickly. 'That sounds like the

bitter voice of experience,' she said, making the statement a gentle invitation to expand on that oblique hint of some sorrow in his life.

As she'd half expected, he didn't take it up.

'There's something else. I know you were hurt when I walked away from you eighteen months ago. I meant to hurt you.' He smiled slightly at her expression. 'It was for your own good, Copleigh. If you were that impressed with my work, it probably meant that you were going to be far too heavily influenced by it. And that wouldn't help you. You'd have to find your own style, your own voice. Without the great Seton Chambers overshadowing whatever talent you had.'

She gaped at him, taken completely by surprise. 'Are you serious?'

'I'm a serious man.'

'And *have* I found my own style and my own voice?'

His lip curled mockingly. 'You may do. In ten or fifteen years' time.'

The cutting reply washed scarlet into her cheeks again. Before she could retort, though, Seton reached out, and to her amazement, ran his fingers through her hair, brushing it back from her high forehead. The touch almost made her cry out. It was so intense that it made her shudder, made her want to arch her neck like a cat under his caress.

The hundred-fathom eyes, dark as the twin barrels of revolvers, looked beneath her own half-closed lids.

'You need some sleep,' he said gently. 'You've been pretending to read that book all night. It's a long way to Katmandu, Copleigh.' He reached up, and flicked off the reading light, plunging her into night.

But sleep had seldom been further from her than now. For the next hour she lay awake, staring with unseeing eyes at the night sky outside. This, the first intimate contact there had ever been between them, had disturbed her in many ways. She almost never spoke about her parents to others—yet with Seton, it had seemed so natural. And his compassion had been warm without sentimentality, giving her a strange sense of comfort. Her own life. He'd been right; her childhood was long gone now, and it was time she began distancing herself from the miseries of her adolescence. Self-pity wouldn't get her anywhere.

His eyes had been so gentle, as if for the first time she could really see into them. Or had that been a trick of the soft light? It was so hard to tell whether there was any real feeling for her behind his sometimes harsh manner, any real appreciation of her as an artist or as a woman . . .

Aware of his presence close beside her, she lay restless and uncertain, haunted by the memory of his casual touch.

CHAPTER FOUR

THE Land Rover slithered across the track, its wheels losing their grip in the mud. Seton muttered a word that might have raised Madge's eyebrows in normal circumstances, but which now echoed her own feelings remarkably well. He slammed the engine into a lower gear, and stamped on the accelerator hard. With a surge, the Land Rover dug its heels into the yeasty red mud and hauled itself back up the steep slope.

At the top of the hill, Madge let out a sigh of relief. Despite the cold, which had made her huddle into her quilted cotton anorak, she was now sweating. A wall of mist and rain swept down the hillside across them, for a moment winning the battle with the windscreen wipers. Seton pulled up and switched off the engine. She glanced at him in surprise.

'Stopping for a rest?'

'No.' He reached behind into the box on the back seat and pulled out the Nagra tape-recorder. 'Get the camera.'

'*The camera?*' She stared at the rain lashing against the windscreen in dismay, but Seton was already outside, pulling the hood of his parka over his face. Muttering, she hauled her camera out of its bag, and with a shudder, opened the door and jumped down on to the road. The mist was thick and white, and she could taste the ice in it. Himalayan breath, she thought.

She scrambled up to where Seton was setting up the microphone.

'Well?' she demanded, her face screwed up against the rain, 'what are we going to shoot?'

'The view.'

'What view?' she demanded acidly. They were in the midst of the Himalayas now. This was the road from Katmandu to Xigaze, the trail that had been trodden over thousands of years by the pilgrims and the traders, the adventurers and the bandits, the holy and the profane, making their way to the sacred city of Lhasa. There would probably be a view, a spectacular one—if they hadn't been in the middle of a driving mist.

Not mist, she thought suddenly. Dear God, this is *cloud*. We're up in the clouds. Literally.

'Let's get back to the car,' she begged him, unable to see his face beneath the hood. 'Please! There's nothing to see——'

'Is your camera ready?'

'For God's sake, Chambers,' she said angrily, losing her patience, 'there's nothing to film, I tell you——'

Abruptly, the mist ahead seemed to glow. For a mad second she thought it must be the headlights of a car approaching, but then she realised it was simply sunlight. Then the thick white cloud tore into rags, and with all the deliberation of a curtain rising, opened to reveal the valley below.

Madge could only gape. The road ahead descended in a long, winding ribbon down the rough hillside, until it was lost among the stunted trees and shrubs that lined it. Beyond, the valley opened out, immense and desolate, a thousand, two thousand feet below. The mountains towered in incomparable majesty along its sides, their steep flanks bare, or veined here and there with snow. The very highest peaks were lost in the dense cloud that soared above, but the whole scene was lit by a lurid, stark light that was somehow in complete harmony with the mood of the scene.

Her hands were shaking as she fumbled with the lens, zooming backwards to take in the whole panorama. She had never seen anything so awesome, so majestic. If only she could get a long enough clip before the cloud descended again——

The almost inaudible whirr of the camera seemed the only sound in that vast solitude. Then, slowly, she became aware of the sound of the wind. Or rather, the sounds. The eerie moan of the wind through the rocks, the rustle of the stubble grass, the soft rush of the high jet-stream above their heads—it was a symphony that played all around them, without end or beginning. Music from the heart of the Himalayas. That was what Seton would be recording—the perfect background to this awe-inspiring view.

She zoomed slowly down the valley, the superb Arco lens almost giving the impression of being in a helicopter, high above the valley floor. Long seconds passed, then the first shreds of cloud began to whip past them. With a sigh, Madge prepared to stop the camera.

'Keep filming,' Seton ordered harshly. She obeyed implicitly, her finger pressed against the button. The cloud sailed in slowly, again with that stunning effect of a curtain being closed. Her mouth curved into a slow smile against the cold aluminium of the camera. He'd been right; this incredibly stagey end to the scene was perfect. The view was almost gone now, the light sinking fast. Carefully, she adjusted the lens to allow for the gathering darkness—and then the white swirl was back, and with it the driving rain.

'Okay.'

She stopped the camera, switched it off, and stood back, shaking her head.

'I've never seen anything like that. Never.' She turned to him, her beautiful eyes soft. 'It was almost as though the mountains arranged that especially for the camera.'

'The Himalayas like to arrange their own publicity,' he said coolly, closing the tape recorder. 'As the daughter of actors, you should appreciate that,

Copleigh.' His eyes met hers stonily, and then he walked back to the Land Rover.

Cheap shot, she thought bitterly, following. Maybe it had been unwise to expose her vulnerability to Seton on the plane two days ago. She'd been crazy to think he cared; he was probably the sort of man who would enjoy jabbing at a sore place out of sheer cussedness.

She hauled herself up into the passenger seat, slamming the door with unnecessary force. The magic of that fabulous moment had evaporated.

'Next time,' Seton said silkily, 'when I say get the camera ready, you do it. Understand?'

'I'm sorry,' she gritted, her tone implying exactly the opposite.

'You missed a good half-minute of that shot.'

'I *said* I'm sorry!' The engine roared, and they jolted back on to the track, the in-car heater beginning to blow deliciously welcome warmth on to her feet again. 'Anyway,' she said snappily, feeling like arguing, 'you can't tell me you knew the mist would part like that. It was sheer coincidence. Or do you,' she suggested sourly, 'have this Moses-like power over the clouds?'

'You're an amusing little super-brat,' he said gently, guiding the slip-sliding Land Rover with powerful hands. 'But don't push it.' She folded her arms into a grumpy knot, and stared out of the window with hot green eyes. 'And don't argue.' She gritted her teeth. 'And fasten your seat-belt.' Go jump, she thought resentfully, not complying.

He steered the powerful vehicle round a tight corner, then went on calmly, 'Until thirty years ago, Copleigh, Tibet was a land without wheels. Know why?' She sat in angry silence. 'Well, it was all to do with some characters known as the Mimyin, the spirits of the earth. They could play hell with a traveller who offended them—and scarring the earth with wheels was a sure way of offending them.'

'Thank you for the lecture in social anthropology,' she said sardonically.

'Anthropology? I'm talking about fact, Copleigh.'

'I suppose you believe in demons, ghosts and wizards?' she said, turning to him with arched eyebrows, the princess to the peasant.

'The Mimyin ruled this country a thousand years before the Buddha, three thousand years before you and me. Take it from me, the Mimyin are probably still going strong.' Just around the bend, a rockfall had half blocked the road, and he braked hard. Madge shot forward off her seat, and slammed painfully against the Land Rover's unyielding dashboard. Winded and bruised, she pushed herself dazedly back into her seat. 'And that's what happens to super-brats who won't fasten their seatbelts,' he purred.

She buckled the belt in a painful silence, hating him.

'You did that on purpose!' she spat out at last, when he had carefully driven round the obstacle.

'I put the brake on,' he agreed. 'But the Mimyin arranged the landslide. And you wouldn't put your seatbelt on. I'd say the blame was fairly evenly spread.' His eyes met hers in the mirror, cold, mocking. 'Wouldn't you?'

She rubbed her tingling elbows, thinking unprintable retorts.

'The question you'll be asking yourself, of course,' he went on calmly, as though there'd been no interruption, 'is how did the Tibetans get around in the bad old days without wheels? Well, they rode on yaks. Or, if they were very rich and important, they rode on humans.'

Despite herself, Madge was intrigued. 'Porters?'

'Slaves, Copleigh, slaves.'

'I reckon I know how the slaves must have felt,' she said tartly.

The Cheshire-cat smile revealed excellent teeth for a second, almost fooling her into believing it was really meant. He took one hand off the wheel to pull a packet of barley-sugar out of the glove compartment. 'Have one.'

'No, thank you.'

'You're tempting the Mimyin again,' he said. Eyes intent on the road ahead, he crunched the splintery candy with relish. She winced at the sound.

'Must you? You must have teeth like nutcrackers! And why am I tempting the leprechauns?'

'At high altitudes it's essential to keep your blood-sugar level up.' He pointed to a dial that had been bolted on to the dashboard. 'Did you think that was a rev counter?'

She looked closer. It was an altimeter. Reading 8,000 feet above sea-level.

Hastily she took a sweet from the bag, and popped it into her mouth.

'The Mimyin will be *so* pleased,' Seton said silkily. The road wound steeply down into the mist and rain below, and he turned his attention to the rebellious wheel of the car. 'From here on,' he said, his eyes careful on the mist ahead, 'the altitude may start affecting you. You can expect a bit of nausea and dizziness at the least, maybe even black-outs and severe pains in your chest and legs.'

'I know what to expect, thank you,' she said shortly.

'You do?'

She met his amused eyes in the mirror, and tried to put on her princess face again.

'You seem to find me very amusing, Chambers.'

'Your self-confidence impresses me,' he drawled. 'It must be something to do with being Tyrone and Olivia Copleigh's daughter.' Madge shot him a dirty look.

'That's unfair, and you know it! Why are you always running me down?'

'I didn't know I was.'

'Well, you are,' she snapped. 'You're cold and mocking. You call me a brat——'

'A super-brat,' he corrected impassively.

'—and keep telling me how inefficient I am.' She clung to the strap beside her as the Land Rover bounced heavily over a series of potholes in the road. 'Why? Do you have to boost your own ego the whole time by putting someone else down? Or is it just me?'

'You flatter yourself, Copleigh.' His sure hands guided the car surely round an awkward bend. 'I don't treat you any different from anyone else.'

'You mean you're this cruel with everyone?' she asked sarcastically.

'Demanding, Copleigh, not cruel. And yes, I'm like this with everyone.'

'Even your nearest and dearest?' she said sweetly.

'Even my nearest and dearest,' he confirmed coolly.

'Is that why your wife——' She bit off the words in horror.

'Why my wife what?' he asked bleakly.

'Nothing,' Madge faltered. What devil had prompted her to bring the subject up? She'd been about to make some taunting remark about his wife's death before sanity had intervened.

Seton pulled the Land Rover up on the road and switched the engine off. In the silence, he turned to Madge with arctic eyes. The colour had drained from her face, leaving it pale and beautiful; but he wasn't interested in her beauty.

'Why my wife *what*?' he repeated, the edge of his voice like a knife. Feeling horribly cornered, Madge looked away from the unbearable anger in his eyes.

'I'm sorry,' she said miserably. 'I don't know what I was going to say. I got carried away in the argument.' She raised her eyes to his. 'I'm sorry,' she said again, feeling helpless. His face was like stone, his jaw clenched so hard that the golden tan was pale around his mouth. For a long minute she cowered internally, expecting him to erupt.

Then he turned back to the wheel, and re-started the Land Rover with a crash of gears. In a dead silence, they drove on into the rain and mist.

Well, Madge thought weakly; grateful that he hadn't chosen to hit back, that settles one question. Whatever the relationship between Seton and Lana Chambers had been, he had definitely been very much in love with her. His reaction made that utterly plain. Man of granite he might be—but he had loved once. A great deal.

For some reason, the thought merely added to her general depression.

Xigaze was silent in the Himalayan night.

The mist and rain had slowly disappeared through the afternoon, and just before sunset, the immense sky had been clear, and for the first time they had had a chance to really assess the landscape around them. They had both been stunned by the harsh yet serene majesty of the mountains that stretched as far as the eye could see from west to east. Just outside Xigaze, they had stopped to film the sun going down, and Madge had seen her first yaks—massive, indomitable creatures rather like bison, but with robes of thick hair that fell around their broad shoulders almost to their knees.

In the room they had had to share, the firelight and the oil-lamp combined to make a soft glow that would have been a lot more suitable for two people who weren't tense and stiff with each other.

Madge nodded as Seton passed the mug of steaming coffee over to her.

'Wow,' she choked, aware of a powerful alcoholic burn all the way down to her stomach, 'what did you put in it?'

'Whisky,' he said succinctly, and poured more coffee into her mug. 'Drink it. It'll help warm you up.'

She obeyed, huddling closer into her down sleeping-bag. The night was bitter cold, and in this village above the tree-line, fuel was practically non-existent. The little fire that crackled in the baked-mud hearth was a rare privilege, they knew. Their host, a local government official, had insisted they take the fuel, blocks of something that looked like peat, and Madge had secretly been nothing loth. The long drive up from Katmandu had been chillingly cold, and the temperature had seemed even lower with the tension that had reigned between them.

She watched Seton as he wrapped the cans of exposed film in their waterproof wrapping. That brief moment of intimacy in the plane seemed never to have happened. Why on earth had she brought up his wife? The argument, though acrimonious, hadn't even been that serious—but mentioning Lana had turned him to stone. Since then, Seton had been icily polite, his thoughts obviously remote. Indifferent to her.

And she had had a recurrence of one of her childhood feelings—the feeling she used to have when her parents, grown bored with her, sent her off to stay with friends. Just for the weekend, the week, the month. Or when they had made it clear she was only in the way of their lives.

But I'm almost twenty-four, she thought in hurt puzzlement. I'm a grown woman. Why does he make me feel so miserable? She so desperately wanted him to acknowledge her as a colleague, maybe even a friend. Friend? He probably had no friends.

If she dug down deep enough, and was truthful enough with herself, what hurt her the most was that he seemed indifferent to her as a woman. He didn't flirt, for example, didn't make the amusing remarks she was used to from men, even from Charlie. He seldom made any concessions to her femininity in the way of especial gentleness or kindness. To some women in the television business, she knew, that sort of thing smacked of old-fashioned chauvinism; they didn't like any suggestion that they were being pampered, or given preferential treatment simply because of being female. With Seton, Madge felt just the other way around—that he was almost deliberately treating her as though she were sexless.

Except that where he was concerned, she was anything but sexless. She almost believed that he made a special point of not seeming interested in her body, her *femininity*, for want of a better word.

Okay, so she wasn't a raving beauty, like her mother. She watched his broad shoulders as he stirred the fire into a brighter blaze. But at least she was a woman. And he was a man—more a man than anyone she had ever known . . .

It was almost as though, for some inner reason, he was grimly determined to avoid any emotional entanglements whatsoever. As though deep inside there was a vulnerability which accounted for the impenetrable masks he had habitually come to wear. Could a man who had lost his wife in tragic circumstances ever recover emotionally? That fierce antagonism to any form of emotional tenderness, she was forced to admit to herself, might be simply because he was still, would always be, in love with Lana. Or because, as he had hinted that night on the plane, of some emotional disaster that had embittered him, made him afraid of love. Seton *afraid*? Was that possible?

'That peat smells good,' she ventured, wanting to get away from her own trapped thoughts.

'It's dried yak-dung.'

'Of course,' she nodded. 'I should have remembered. There wouldn't be any peat up here.'

He nodded slightly. The fragrant, sweet smell was almost a kind of incense. The Chinese authorities, Madge remembered having read, had tried to persuade the Tibetans to use coal, so that the yak-dung could be used as precious fertilizer, but they had complained that they couldn't stand the smell of the coal-smoke.

Her green eyes, their pupils big and dark in the soft light, followed him as he sat down on his own bunk-bed, parallel to hers—though chastely separated by a large oxygen cylinder—and ran his hands tiredly through his thick, dark hair.

He must be exhausted, she thought, after that terrible drive. There were shadows of weariness under his eyes, and by the way he kept stretching his shoulders, he'd strained his neck at the wheel.

Acting on an irresistible impulse, she slid her legs out of her sleeping-bag, stepped over to him, and kissed him quickly on the corner of his mouth. He looked up at her in surprise, and she smiled timidly.

'That's just to say thank you for getting us here safely,' she said softly. 'And—sorry for being so childish this afternoon.' She scrambled back into her bag, wondering whether she was about to receive the snub of a lifetime.

But when she eventually had the courage to look back at him, he was calmly unlacing his mountain boots, as though nothing had happened. She smiled ruefully to herself. What did you expect, Madge? Some kind of immediate détente?

Seton zipped himself into his sleeping-bag—an Arctic one, she noticed with envy—and lay back on the narrow bolster, his dark eyes staring up into the soft gloom of the ceiling, where the firelight was casting a flickering light. What a strange situation this was, she thought. In a strange land, in a strange house, sleeping in a little room with Seton Chambers, her one-time idol and now hostile partner.

Fleetingly, the thought occurred to her that her attitude towards Seton had undergone a mysterious alteration. Her old hostility towards him was still there—but not constantly. It rose up in flashes, now and then, as it had done this afternoon. And in between—in between was a confused area of emotion she hardly understood. She knew only that it hurt most of the time, that it was compounded out of anxiety, awe, and a burning desire to be recognised by him.

She shied away from probing these feelings too deeply. They were crazy, in any case, on an important assignment like this one. And instead, her thoughts reached out to that other woman who had lain in Seton's bed, who had loved him, and who—perhaps— had known him better than any other human being. Lana. A shadowy figure, about whom all she knew was that she had been a model, had been full of life, and had died suddenly and violently in a car crash. Another statistic. What had she been like? Had she loved him as much as he evidently had loved her?

She closed her eyes, the sweet smell of the fire haunting her.

'Who told you about Lana?' His deep voice blended so accurately with her thoughts that she answered without hesitation.

'Dennis Quinton. And all he said was that she'd been killed——' She bit her lip. 'Had died—in a car crash.' She looked across at him, thinking how pagan he seemed in the firelight, how utterly male. And how remote from her. 'Seton——' It was only the second time she had used his name, and it sounded awkward on her lips. '—I'm so sorry about this afternoon. I—I didn't mean to upset you . . .'

'It's not important.' He sighed tiredly. 'It was just a bit of a shock to hear Lana mentioned. Most people don't even talk about her to me. I guess they're afraid I'll hit the roof. At one time, maybe I would have done.'

'I thought you were going to this afternoon,' she ventured.

He shrugged slightly. 'What the hell, anyway. It seems a long time ago now.'

'Five years,' she said.

'Is it?' He smiled tightly, wryly, in a way she had never seen him do before. 'You seem remarkably well informed about my private history.'

'That's just what Dennis said,' she ventured.

'Dennis liked her,' he nodded slowly. 'Everyone liked Lana. She was bright, beautiful. She was easy to love.'

'I'm sorry,' she said again. 'I didn't mean to trespass on something private.'

His deep eyes lost their focus, and Madge wasn't sure whether he was listening to her. 'Something private,' he repeated in a murmur. 'Lana wasn't a private woman. Not many models are. They can't take too much privacy, too much shade. They get hungry for the spotlights and the lenses. But she was lovely—tall and slender, like a young willow tree. Her eyes were almost the same colour as yours.' He glanced at her face briefly. 'Like cloudy emeralds.' As though made restless by his thoughts, he sat upright, and stared into the fire. 'Lana wanted to be in the movies, Copleigh. She wanted to be a star, like Monroe, Bardot, all the other blonde dreams. She was blonde, with hair like spun gold, and skin like honey.'

Madge hugged her knees, feeling very small and plain and dull.

'What happened?' she asked.

'What usually happens,' he said bitterly. The first emotion she had ever seen on his face was now flickering with the firelight in his eyes. 'She became obsessed with the idea, and nothing could stop her. I took her with me to Africa, but she hated the silence and the wildness. We went to the Riviera, gambled in Monte Carlo, skiied in Biarritz . . . She couldn't get the dream out of her head. We always ended up back in England or California. Screen tests, meetings with directors, days and weeks of depression.' A hard gust of wind moaned at the shuttered windows, for a moment reminding them both of the Himalayan night outside. Then the midnight-blue eyes were again staring back into the luxurious desolation of Los Angeles days. 'There was only one flaw in the dream, Copleigh. Lana wasn't an actress. She'd been a successful model, and she was stunningly photogenic; but as soon as she moved or opened her mouth, she revealed herself for what she was—a nice girl. A nice girl who didn't have a snowball's chance in hell of becoming an actress. She even landed tiny parts in various films now and then— but she was so bad that they'd edit those sections out before the film was released.'

'And she'd be shattered?' Madge guessed quietly. She knew it all so well, knew the tragedy of people like Lana Chambers. Anyone who had been in the movie world knew about people like Lana.

'Completely,' he nodded. 'It was a neurosis with her, a compulsion. Something one couldn't explain. It had always been there, its roots deep in her unconscious, like some alien thing inside her. Another Lana, one who could dominate the woman I'd married at any time.'

'Wouldn't a psychiatrist have helped?' Madge asked quietly.

'Los Angeles psychiatrists!' He laughed softly, without amusement. 'She went through six. And still the illness was growing. It was eating her away inside, leaving nothing but a shell. She was drinking heavily from the start—but at the end she lived on nothing but alcohol and pills. And I couldn't help. I couldn't help, and I couldn't stand it. I tried for three years, but it was no good. And in the end, I just opted out—after three years of marriage. I left Lana with the other Hollywood crazies, the pschiatrists and the so-called friends who kept egging her on, eager to see her destroyed because they were jealous of her beauty and the happiness she once had. I buried myself in my work. I took a schooner from Miami to Newfoundland, chasing the great whales all the way. I made *The Whale's Song* that summer. When I got back, Lana was worse than ever. Our marriage——'

Again, that chilling laugh. 'We didn't have a marriage. She was having an affair with a director, a man in his sixties, who'd promised to make her a star. She was too drugged, too neurotic to see through him. I went out to Alaska to make a film about the oil pipeline and the men who worked on it. Then I came back to California—not to L.A., but to 'Frisco, somewhere I could be near Lana, but not too near to hurt either of us. She came to see me in the fall.' Wearily, he rubbed his eyes, his mouth harsh. Aching for him, Madge sat in silence, understanding far more than he could ever know, anticipating what was to come next. 'There's a highway between Los Angeles and San Francisco, Copleigh. Almost five hundred miles long. Sometimes you can see the Pacific stretching away on your left all the way to the other side of the world. She got fifty miles along it before she found what she was looking for. A place where the road ran high and narrow, where you could see the ocean and the sky and the mountains. All the things she'd loved before her illness blinded her for ever to anything but her dreams. It must have taken courage to twist the wheel, because they didn't find any pills or alcohol in her blood. She was stone-cold sober as she dropped a thousand feet down into the valley.'

'Maybe it was an accident,' Madge said gently. 'You can't know she meant to take her life——'

'I know what she meant,' he said quietly, silencing her. His face was a mask, his eyes full of pain. 'She told me that's how she would do it, long ago. And I abandoned her. I left her with her illness and her pathos and her suffering, and closed my mind.'

'What else could you do?' Madge pleaded, his pain frightening her. 'It wasn't your fault, Seton. I know movie people—the failures as well as the successes. I've lived with them all my life. And there's nothing you can do to change them.' He closed his eyes, lying back against the bolster, deep lines incised into the weatherbeaten gold of his face. For the second time that night, she struggled out of her sleeping-bag, wanting to cry. She knelt on the cold floor beside him, her fingers biting into the hard muscle of his arm.

'Seton—I *know*! Don't you think I've had some insight into that world? My parents are exactly the same as Lana was. The only difference is that they had talent, they've been successful. But they're exactly the same, eaten up inside by their compulsions, unable to live or love outside of a studio. But if they'd been unable to make it, they'd have come to the same end. I know that, deep in my heart.' Her voice was urgent, vibrant with passion, and he opened his eyes slowly to stare into hers. 'It *is* an illness,' she went on, more gently. 'An illness that eventually destroys everything that's real and genuine in their natures, leaving them hollow, selfish. Brittle. Ready to crumble at the slightest knock. Very, very few escape that sickness, only the strong, the good. The others get eaten up by it, like an addiction— and it's the same whether they're mega-stars or failures. You can't blame yourself for the rest of your life for what happened. It was fated. Lana would have come to the same sad end whether you'd been there or not.'

'She died because I neglected her,' he said softly.

'*No!* She died for herself, Seton. Not for you. I can't bear to see you like this—it wasn't your fault, I know it wasn't!'

His eyes searched hers for a long minute, their power almost tangible. Then he prised her fingers off his arm with gentle, strong fingers, and raised her so that she was sitting beside him.

'You think you know, little one?' As he had done last night, his fingers combed through her coppery hair, brushing the curls away from her forehead. It was a dizzying, sweet caress that was over even as she swayed towards him. 'Maybe you do, at that. Maybe you do.' He leaned back, studying her wryly. 'If you think I'm a cold bastard, Madge, that I treat you harshly—just remember what I've told you tonight. And try to understand why I need to keep you at a distance.' She bit her lip hard, closing her eyes. 'I sometimes get asked why I don't make films about people any more,' he went on gently. 'I think you can guess the reason now. I prefer the simplicity, the unchangeability, maybe even the savagery, of nature. The same applies to the relationships I have with women. I keep them as physical as I can. Physical, with no hope of any sentimental developments, ever. You understand that?' She nodded silently, wondering with a tearing twist of pain whether she would ever be able to accept him on those stark terms. He leaned forward, and her lips parted helplessly, as though for his kiss.

It didn't come. The warmth in those ultramarine depths cooled slowly, and the wry smile faded from his mouth. 'There are very few women who can handle that kind of relationship, Madge. And I don't believe you're one of them. Maybe you think I'm immoral, but I play this game to very strict rules. The first one is that if there's the slightest chance of either of us getting hurt, the whole idea is off. In this situation,' he said quietly, 'there's every chance that both of us would get hurt very badly indeed. That's been obvious from the very beginning, and you know it as well as I do.' She nodded again, fighting her impulse to argue with him. She'd only get mercilessly snubbed for her pains. 'And now it's bedtime,' he said gently. 'We've got a fifty-mile drive to Lhasa facing us tomorrow morning.' She found herself firmly pushed to her own bed.

As she slid into her sleeping-bag, Seton blew the oil-lamp's soft flame out, and they were left in the flickering cave-light of the fire. In silence, Madge squeezed her eyes shut, remembering that brief, intoxicating caress. That was twice he had touched her. Twice in a year and a half. At least she now had been given a piercing insight into the reasons why.

Did he have any idea, she wondered ironically, what he did to her? Of course he did. What he had just said to her made it obvious that he saw all too clearly into her heart.

But it didn't help the deep ache inside her to know that he was trying to protect her from terrible hurt. She desired him, physically, with a frighteningly deep passion. The merest brush of Seton's fingers could set her aflame as Andrew Everett's lovemaking had never done. But he had been right—she wanted more than that out of a relationship. She wanted love, above all. The one thing that Seton couldn't, wouldn't give.

Strange how she was coming to understand him. He was unfolding for her, slowly but surely. Coming closer, yet paradoxically, further away. She was beginning to see into the man he really was, see past the golden masks he wore; and yet the more she saw of him, the more she saw that might keep them apart for ever . . .

'Don't think.' The command cut into her thoughts. 'Just sleep.' And for once, she wanted to obey, didn't want to have any other thought but the memory of the way his fingers had touched her. With an effort of will, she disengaged her thoughts and waited for sleep to come and bury her, with all her doubts and confusions and all the new knowledge whirling in her head.

Madge, she thought dimly as sleep crept on her. At least he called me Madge.

CHAPTER FIVE

MADGE knew she would never forget her first view of Lhasa.

Like Athens, the city was dominated by a huge outcrop of high white rock in its midst. And from that height, soaring above the ancient stone buildings of the city, stood the Potala, the legendary palace of the Dalai Lamas.

Nothing could have prepared her for this, not all her reading nor all the photographs she had consulted. It was a sight which, after their long pilgrimage here, struck her almost as it must have struck those Buddhist pilgrims hundreds of years ago, who braved the Himalayas, the snow, the bandits, the treachery of the Mimyin, to set eyes on this great shrine.

Seton stopped the Land Rover on the edge of People's Park, and together they stared up at the vision across the lake, oblivious to the inquisitive Tibetans passing by.

The Potala. It could have been nothing but a fortress-monastery; the myriad regularly-spaced windows in its massive white façade spoke of the thousands who had spent so many centuries of prayer and study here. The central section, a deep reddish-pink, rose above the rest, its golden roof sending a blade of light into the milky blue dome of the sky. Immense stone staircases climbed up from ground level to the slowly-tapering peaks of the palace, and they could see tiny human figures clambering up and down, ants on a wedding-cake.

Gradually she allowed her eyes to wander beyond, to the vast semi-circle of mountains that stood around Lhasa valley, their grey peaks cradling this fabulous site.

'The Dalai Lamas were kings as well as gods,' Seton said gently. 'Like the Egyptian Pharaohs. And sometimes they behaved more like kings than like gods.' He glanced at her with that Cheshire-cat smile. 'So don't be all that overawed, Copleigh. This place has seen more intrigue, murder, secrecy and plotting than half a dozen other palaces put together.' He looked back up at the massive presence hanging over them. 'Still, it's a magnificent sight.'

'It's stunning,' she agreed. 'Maybe it's the altitude, but I think it's one of the most wonderful things I've ever seen.'

'I take it you don't regret coming?' he asked.

'I've never regretted coming,' she said quietly. He smiled, and stretched his shoulders. The smile became a grimace, and he arched his head back.

'Anything wrong?' she asked.

'Land Rover neck,' he said ruefully. 'It comes from driving too far over rough terrain.'

'I should have shared the driving,' she said remorsefully. 'Want an aspirin?'

He shook his head, and started the engine. They were expected at the official guest-house which was, Madge knew, the only hotel or restaurant in the whole of Lhasa. Fascinated, she stared out of the window at the thronged streets as they drove there. Cars were scarcely in evidence at all, but the paved streets were busy with Tibetans on foot, most dressed in the blue smock-suits that the Chinese had made so universally popular. Some, though, wore traditional peasant costume, with turned-up yak leather boots which delighted Madge. To her they seemed a happy, inquisitive people, their broad, often disarmingly innocent faces tanned and ruddy-cheeked.

The city itself was, as she had anticipated, clearly mediaeval, most of its buildings and streets obviously hundreds of years old. New sections, though, of modern houses and public buildings had been added by the Chinese, and rather to her relief, the Lhasa Guest House was a modern, comfortable-looking place in one of the newer quarters.

A portly, middle-aged Chinese woman in a grey smock-suit was waiting for them at the reception.

'Mr and Mrs Chambers?'

'Mr Chambers,' Seton corrected, 'and Miss Copleigh.'

'Forgive me,' the woman smiled, her round face creasing in a smile that showed excellent white teeth. She shook them both neatly and lightly by the hand with cool fingers. 'I am Mrs Wong, your guide in Lhasa. Welcome to Tibet.'

They signed the register, gave their passports to the desk-clerk, and followed the solicitous Mrs Wong to the stairs. 'A large party of tourists from the People's Republic has just left,' she informed them. 'But we get very few visitors from the West, still fewer film people. You had a good journey?'

'Rather tiring,' Madge admitted with a weary smile.

'Ah. You would have been more comfortable in the airplane, perhaps,' Mrs Wong suggested, leading them up to their suite. 'Almost all our foreign visitors come by airplane from the Republic—but since you wanted to film the journey from Nepal, you are one of the few parties permitted to drive over the border from the south. You found the Himalayas inspiring?'

'When the mist lifted,' Seton nodded. 'It rained most of the way, unfortunately——'

'Hold on!' Madge gasped, stopping at the landing and putting down her bag. There seemed to be no breath in her lungs, and odd black patches were dancing before her eyes.

'The altitude,' said Seton, quickly taking her arm as she swayed against him. 'Take it easy—just get your breath back, Copleigh.'

'We climbed too fast,' Mrs Wong said apologetically. 'You will have to take care, Miss Copleigh, young as you are. Our air is thin up here, and not to be trifled with. Okay?' Her slanting eyes were concerned as she took Madge's other arm. Together the two of them led her down the corridor to the suite they would be sharing.

There was an oxygen cylinder between the beds in the bedroom—Madge was just beginning to understand the need for this common feature of Tibetan life—and after a few deep breaths from the mouthpiece, her nausea receded quickly. Feeling rather foolish, she twisted the valve shut.

'Sorry,' she mumbled. 'I don't know how that happened.'

'It's I who should be sorry,' said Seton, his eyes worried. 'I shouldn't have set such a pace up those stairs. Feeling better?'

'Much,' she nodded, but despite her smile, didn't try and get up yet.

'In that case,' Mrs Wong said, 'I shall leave you to unpack and rest yourselves. They will send some tea up in a few minutes. Okay?' She beamed at them. 'I shall be waiting to guide you round the Potala tomorrow morning. Oh, and dinner is at seven-thirty.' The door closed noiselessly behind her.

'Sure you're all right?' Seton asked, his dark eyes serious.

'Sure,' Madge said firmly, and cautiously stood up to prove it.

Satisfied that she wasn't going to faint away, Seton went in search of the bathroom to sluice his face. Their suite was small but comfortable, its floor covered with thick Tibetan rugs, and the rooms divided by heavy velvet curtains—both designed, Madge guessed, to keep out the cold. Despite the luxurious touches—plump Chinese-style chairs and couches and feather mattresses on the beds—the suite reminded her strongly of camp accommodation she had had in Africa. There were the same iron bedsteads, the same slightly Spartan neatness to everything. She guessed this functionalism would be the style of modern China.

As they unpacked, she realised that she hadn't considered the fact that they would be sharing a bedroom until now. She glanced surreptitiously at the chastely separated single beds. The urbane Mrs Wong hadn't commented on this, nor had Seton. Sleeping would obviously be all right. But dressing? She resolved to dress in the bathroom during their stay in Lhasa.

She looked at the shut bathroom door, and hastily kicked off her shoes and jeans. Padding across the room in her briefs, she picked a roomy skirt out of the jumble of her clothes in the cupboard, and tied it on. It was delicious to feel cool air around her slender legs after the long drive from Xigaze.

None of this tension had arisen with Charlie. With Charlie there had been no embarrassment about things like the problems of nudity, or her panties and bras drying all over the room. When she wanted to dress, he would simply turn his back, and vice versa. There had never been the slightest hint of sexual tension between, only some very mild jokes they shared.

That sort of relationship was important if you were going to obey the ancient Studio Seven ground rule, that camera teams abroad shared rooms wherever possible to cut costs. She smiled to herself. Now that Studio Seven had made it to the top, that sort of economising would probably disappear for good. Think of yourself as a pioneer, Copleigh!

'Stick to the hot-water tap,' Seton commented, coming back into the little bedroom. 'The cold water's melted ice.' Then, as though he had been sharing her thoughts, his eyes probed hers.

'Do you object to sharing a room with me, Copleigh?'

'Of course not,' she said, too hastily. 'Charlie and I always shared rooms on location.'

'No maidenly reserve?'

'None.' She tried to look cool as she snapped her suitcase shut, and pushed it under her bed. 'We used to share everything.'

'Everything?' Dark eyebrows arched mockingly. 'Lucky Charlie!'

'Everything except that,' she snapped. He was still flexing his shoulders, and she bit her temper back. 'Is your neck still hurting?'

'Like hell,' he confirmed shortly. 'You don't know anything about massage, do you?'

'I used to rub my mother's shoulders when she got tense,' Madge said tentatively, 'I don't know if I could do any good.'

'I'll try anything,' he decided brusquely. 'The last thing I want is a ricked neck at this stage.' To her dismay, he unzipped his heavy anorak and hauled off the khaki shirt he had been wearing. Instinctively, Madge turned her back, her mouth suddenly dry. Her mind's eye held an image of golden skin and hard muscle, an image she remembered all too vividly from that miserable evening of their departure. Except that this wasn't a dream, but the man himself.

'For God's sake, Copleigh,' he said acidly, 'I've only taken my shirt off.' Blushing at her own stupidity, she forced herself to turn to him.

'Where does it hurt?'

'From between my shoulderblades to the back of my neck,' he said, and sat down on the edge of the bed. Her heart beating unevenly, Madge clambered on to the quilt and sat cross-legged behind him. Dear heaven, he was magnificent! Every muscle in his torso was perfectly defined, the smooth skin tanned to a deep gold. She was almost shocked by the dark hair tapering from his chest down to his lean, flat stomach. Or the overwhelming sense of power in his shoulders and arms, where the muscles and tendons moved sleekly beneath the skin.

There were also two silvery star-shaped scars on his left flank. Bullet wounds? He had been in so many wars that she wouldn't have been surprised. She bit her full lower lip with sharp teeth. Was it the altitude making her feel so lightheaded? Her hands were trembling as she laid them uncertainly between his broad shoulderblades.

'Here?' she whispered.

Seton nodded. She took a shaky breath, and pushed against the muscle. His skin was warm velvet, and the muscles beneath were not, as she had imagined, unyielding—but taut, full of a hard, springy life.

'Harder,' he commanded. 'Use your thumbs.' She pushed as hard as she could, and felt the rigid bars of tension among the broad muscles. 'That's where it hurts,' he nodded. She leaned forward, and concentrated on trying to ease the contracted tendons out of their spasm. Seton hung his head forward, his shoulders relaxing under her fingers.

Her hands seemed so pale and small against his back! She slid her palms up the deltoid muscles, the two thick cables that ran from the top of his shoulders to the sides of his neck, assessing their strength. The only other man's body she had known, Andrew's, had been delicate, white, a million miles from this sun-kissed grandeur. Nor, she acknowledged unhappily, had it ever affected her in this startlingly direct way. Her naked knee touched the warmth of his skin, and she drew it away hastily.

Funny—she had always been scornful about he-men, had always been faintly disgusted by the oiled bodies of weight-trainers. But Seton wasn't like that. He was poised, graceful. The set of his body revealed a fiercely proud spirit without vanity or selfconsciousness.

'Is this helping?' she asked, her voice dry in her throat. His deep 'Mmm' of appreciation didn't assist in lowering her pulse-rate. She felt dizzy, a languor creeping slowly over her, and she shook her coppery head to clear it. But being so close to him was intoxicating, like hot wine. Her thoughts flitted briefly to Lana. Did you do this for him? she wondered. And did it make you feel like this? Poor Lana, wherever you are, I hope you're at peace now ... She pressed her palms against the knotted muscle, willing it to ease and relax. Seton, my love, you're so tense. If only I could show you that you aren't to blame, that there was nothing you could have done ...

Giddily, Madge was aware that her massage was becoming a slow, sensual caress, any medicinal intention now disappearing rapidly. Yet she couldn't stop herself, couldn't prevent her hungry fingers from spreading in a delicious exploration of Seton's skin. *Stop*, she commanded herself in a silent gasp, *stop this now, Madge!* But she couldn't. As though there were some irresistible magnetism in him, she sank forward against his back with long lashes fluttering closed over drugged eyes, her cheek resting against the warm skin. Her arms crept round his shoulders, holding him close, and the musky smell of his skin enveloped her.

He turned powerfully, breaking her embrace, and gripped her arms in hands like steel. She clung to his hard forearms, not daring to open her eyes. The stubborn line of her mouth had softened into a voluptuous surrender, her lips half open, their shell-pink stark against the pearly whiteness of her face.

'For the love of God,' he muttered roughly, 'what are you trying to do, Madge?'

'I don't know,' she whispered. 'I'm sorry——'

His mouth was shockingly harsh against her own, his lips forcing hers apart with a pain she welcomed, drank in as a dying woman would drink sweet water. There was no room for doubt, no room for anything but the terrible hunger that locked them together. It obliterated every thought, every feeling but the contact of their bodies and minds in this consuming embrace. Her fingers were clenched in Seton's dark hair, his arms crushing her slender body against the naked power of his chest.

She could taste the sweet urgency of his tongue against hers, could taste the blood from her own cut lip—and then he tore away from her, leaving her shuddering and bereft.

'This is insane,' he said, his deep voice rough and uneven. The muscles of his stomach were in rigid relief as he sucked air into his lungs. She looked up helplessly into the stormy blue depths of his eyes, her lips bruised from his kiss, her whole body aching for him. 'Don't look at me like that,' he said huskily. The passionate curve of his mouth tightened into anger, and he spun away. 'Damn you, Madge! *Don't!*'

In the electric silence, she tried to recover her sanity, running her fingers shakily through the glinting curls of her hair.

When at last he turned to face her, there was a frightening authority in the dark line of his brows.

'That was our first and last slip. We're not going to let it happen again. Understand? The next time that happens, I'm putting you on the first plane home, and I'll make this film on my own.'

'But——'

'That's all.' His voice was like a lash. 'You don't have to like it. That's just the way it is.'

Her emotions still churning inside, Madge stood up.

'Are you trying to tell me that you didn't want that?' she demanded angrily. 'That what happened was nothing to do with you?'

'What happened was a very bad mistake,' he said roughly. 'Repeating it won't do either of us any good.

Emotion and accuracy don't mix. So we're not going to repeat it. And that's all.'

'I see.' She took a deep breath, her eyes avoiding his naked torso. From the whirlpool of her feelings, resentment rose up sharply. 'Emotion is always a mistake in your book, isn't it?'

He ignored the remark.

'We don't even know each other, let alone like each other. But armed hostility is at least better than an infatuation brought on by nothing more than close proximity!' He went on more gently, 'No professional can afford passionate involvements with colleagues, Copleigh. It's lethal—especially in the face of important work needing total dedication.'

'Yes,' she said bitterly, 'the film. Nothing comes before films in your life, does it? Mere human feelings are nothing compared to two hours of prime television time!'

'You're being hysterical,' he said quietly.

'And you're inhuman,' she retorted. 'You talk about "involvement" as though it were some kind of disease!' She tried to gulp down the tears. 'Can't you see that people have emotions, might be vulnerable, easily hurt——'

'By "people" I take it you mean yourself?' he asked. His mouth quirked cynically. 'I didn't suspect you were such a prey to emotionalism, Copleigh. I might have guessed, though. It's the universal failing of super-brats.'

She snatched up the pillow and hurled it at him. He swatted it aside.

'I thought by now you'd got the message,' he snapped. 'You don't like me and I don't like you. But we've got to get this job done. And if we can't do it the easy way, we'll do it the hard way.'

'You're the coldest man I've ever met!'

'It's the way I am,' he said grimly, the set of his mouth forbidding.

'And it's just too bad for the people around you,' Madge went on fiercely, the fire in her veins thickening to ice. 'Like it was too bad about Lana.'

For a second she thought he was going to lash out at her, but the tracery of muscle across his chest merely tightened, his eyes glinting with deep-sea fire.

'That's right,' he said, his voice soft, dangerous. 'You are getting the message, after all.'

There was a tap at the door, and Madge tore her angry eyes away from his. Seton swept up his anorak, zipped it closed over his naked skin, and swung the door open.

An elderly Tibetan smilingly brought in a tray of tea and almond biscuits, and bowed himself out.

Suddenly afraid of her own turbulent emotions, Madge stalked to the bathroom, and slammed the door shut behind her.

'And I don't want any damned tea!' she called tearfully.

Sitting on the edge of the bath, she bowed her head in her hands, and felt the tears creep under her tightly-shut lids.

Damn him! Damn this whole wretched trip! What had gone wrong with her? She wiped the tears away, aching for home. She was wishing she'd never come, wishing she'd let herself be warned off that day in Seton's office.

Her emotions didn't seem able to stay on the level. She was up and down, like a yo-yo . . .

Nervous exhaustion and the altitude were making her giddy again, and she splashed her face with the painfully cold water from the tap, and waited for the nausea to recede. She felt as though she'd been through a mangle, as though every one of her emotions had been bruised and sprained.

Why couldn't she just stay neutral towards Seton? The way her emotions swung wildly from one extreme to another frightened her. Last night she had felt so close to him, felt she understood so much about him. This afternoon she had veered from an overwhelming desire to a kind of unbalanced hatred of him. Remembering the way her body had just melted against his, she shook her head in despair.

Like a cat on heat. But even in this miserable, cold afterwards, Madge knew she couldn't have stopped herself. There had been no choice involved—touching Seton had been a compulsion. And the way her nerves felt now, it was soon going to be an addiction—for nothing but his touch, she was certain, could drive away this sick ache inside. Did she have any more control over her moods and movements than any other satellite, caught in the magnetism of a planet? Did the moon ever long to be free of the earth, the way she was longing now?

Dully, she switched on the bath, and watched the hot water pour into the massive tub. A long soak might take away some of this misery. As the steam filled the bathroom, she pulled her hair into a little pigtail and stripped off her clothes, letting them fall casually on to the floor. She felt like a bit of slovenly relaxation right now!

Confused as her mind might be, though, the evidence of her body's voluptuous arousal was unambiguous to her touch. Hating her own sexuality for the first time in her life, she clambered into the too-hot water and sank down gratefully.

And waited for the heat to soak away her desire and her ache, her mind numb.

'And this,' Mrs Wong said, 'is the sepulchre of the Fifth Dalai Lama.' Light-meter in hand, Madge stared up at the jewel-encrusted structure, its solid gold spire lost high in the gloom above. So much gold, she thought, so many jewels . . .

They had seen enough marvels this morning to fill a dozen museums—great altars loaded with offerings and the ubiquitous silken scarves that were a part of any Buddhist ritual here in Tibet; countless golden statues of the Lamas, guarded by fearsome deities, and some reputed to be thousands of years old; exquisite brocades and drapes and murals—the Potala was one of the world's great treasure-houses.

'The title "Dalai Lama", of course, means "Ocean of Wisdom",' Mrs Wong went on, watching Seton as he scanned the great chamber with his hand-lens, planning the shots to come. Later today, he and Madge were going to start filming inside the Potala, and he was already mapping out the scenes they would take. It was almost lunchtime, and Madge was starving. Only a few more rooms to go. 'The Dalai Lama was the temporal as well as the spiritual ruler of Tibet, with absolute power over the people, who have always been extremely poor.' She smiled. 'Okay? The Lamas taxed the Tibetan people very heavily for many centuries to assemble all this wealth.' She waved a neat hand at the treasures all around, her almond eyes reflecting the polite incomprehension of a secular mind faced with extravagant displays of religious belief.

It was indeed, Madge thought, almost beyond belief that so poor a people as the Tibetans had put up with an iron-fisted religious despotism with sometimes savage laws and punishments, and merciless taxes, for so many centuries.

'It's a paradox,' Seton mused, echoing her thoughts. In the soft light, his eyes were almost black. 'So many wonders here, such immense spirituality—and yet such misery outside these walls. People starving, prepared to live in abject misery in expectation of the world to come.' Mrs Wong nodded vigorously, and launched into a long catalogue of the horrors of Lamaism, interspersing her comments with the occasional, 'Okay?'

Madge wondered, with some amusement, where their charming guide had picked up this Americanism.

But Madge couldn't rid herself of a feeling of awe in this place, a feeling that great holiness and mercy—as well as primitive brutality—had existed in this fabulous fortress. They moved onwards into the Hall of Western Sunshine, still listening to Mrs Wong.

As they passed through the doorway, her arm bumped Seton's, and she flinched away. Since the disastrous events of yesterday, she had been incredibly awkward with him, avoiding those deep blue eyes and wincing at every chance contact, as though his body were white-hot to her touch. For his part, he had simply ignored her, as he was doing now, his face back in its golden mask.

Like the golden masks of the priest-kings in their shrines all around. Madge glanced behind her quickly. It was easy, in this shadowy place, to imagine that there were supernatural presences in the darkness. Several times already she had 'seen' dim figures at the edge of her vision, and had spun round to find no one there.

The Hall of Western Sunshine, despite its name, was as shadowy a hall as the others. Madge wandered slowly past a magnificent row of carved and painted wooden pillars, letting Seton and the Chinese guide go on ahead. It was so quiet here, so peaceful. Over everything hung the heavy smell of a thousand flickering yak-butter lamps, their yellow flames visible in front of every shrine or statue. Despite the influence of Maoism on everyday life in Tibet, many had stayed faithful to the Buddhism in which they and their ancestors had been born.

She glanced at the grotesque shadows cast by the lamps, and at the glaring eyes of the fiends and protective monsters all around, and reflected that Tibetan Buddhism counted some horrible conceptions among its pantheon. Mrs Wong's fluting voice drifted down the colonnade from up ahead. To her, as to the other Chinese administrators, religion meant little. Madge paused to stare at the dragons and monsters that writhed in painted fury up the satin brocade beside her. A slight draught made the material stir, so that the savage eyes and lolling tongues seemed for an instant alive. With a shudder, she turned away.

The impression of people all around her, at the periphery of her vision, was difficult to shake off. She kept 'seeing' groups of two or three Lamas from the corner of her eye, complete with their brown robes and shaven heads; but whenever she turned, smiling, there were only the shadows and the golden idols to mock her.

It was an eerie feeling. With the hairs on the back of her neck prickling, she looked up for Seton. Neither he nor Mrs Wong were in sight, though she could hear the woman's voice echoing from somewhere far off.

'Damn,' she whispered. The guide had warned them about getting lost in the maze-like halls of the Potala. She glanced uncertainly around, wondering whether to call. Somehow, the thought of desecrating this mysterious silence was too much for her. Compressing her lips into a determined line, she walked back the way she had come, a slender, graceful figure amidst the ancient gloom.

The trouble was that the ornate exits all looked alike to her—and there were nine hundred and ninety-nine rooms in this palace. Mrs Wong's voice now seemed further off than ever. Which way now? From the entrance of a sacred chamber, a monstrous deity glared at her, his three bloodshot eyes and gaping fangs towering down from under a massive golden crown. She stopped, and looked around unhappily. She had never been superstitious, but she could think of better places to get lost in than the Potala. And her heart was beating unevenly, a sign that the lack of oxygen was affecting her. If she wasn't careful, she was going to have another fainting fit.

Now thoroughly upset, she pushed through the doorway beside her. No sign of the others. But here, at least, someone had recently been, for a row of yak-butter lamps were flickering brightly before a towering golden Buddha. She looked away from the shrine—and blinked at yet another monk.

But there could be no mistake this time. That was a *real* Lama! She waited in silence as the saffron-robed monk arranged a bowl of flowers before the great Buddha of Compassion. He was old, his face fallen into patient lines, and Madge could see his hands tremble slightly as he touched the fresh spring flowers. Where, she wondered vaguely, had he found spring flowers in midsummer? Perhaps he grew them himself, in honour of the Buddha. She watched him, thinking of all the thousands of men like this one who had tended this palace and its deities over the centuries. What would he make of the Chinese administration and its secular outlook? She noticed the darns and patches on his robe, the shabbiness of his curled boots. He would certainly not speak English, she knew, but he would be able to guess she was lost, and lead her to Seton.

The Lama pressed his palms together before the shrine and bowed. Then, gathering his robe, he turned to Madge. A beaming smile crossed his ancient face as he saw her. Smiling in return, she stepped forward.

'Excuse me——'

The words froze in her throat.

He was gone. He had simply melted away before her eyes, she had even seen the lamp-flames behind appear through his transparent body. Madge gaped at the bowl.

The flowers in it were withered and dusty, and the spring they had bloomed in had been dead for decades.

She spun away from the silent shrine, her scalp prickling in horror, and ran terrified into the darkness beyond, sending a tray of brass cups crashing to the ground as she went.

The clatter was like iron feet in pursuit. Her heart was pounding in her throat, the air thin and cold in her lungs. All she could think of was escape, escape from smiling Lamas who weren't there and spring flowers that had been dead for years. Sobbing and giddy, she burst through the red leather door in her way—and screamed sharply as she cannoned into Seton's hard chest.

As his arms came around her in blissful protection, she sank forward with wet eyes, close to fainting.

'Damn it, Copleigh,' he cursed, 'what the hell are you playing at?'

'A Lama,' she stammered, clinging to him with desperate fingers. 'I saw a Lama in the hall—and when I spoke to him, he just vanished——'

'Take it easy,' he said, more gently.

'But I *saw* him,' she pleaded. 'It wasn't a mistake! He was there! I saw his face and his robes, even the patches on his boots——'

'It isn't unusual for such things to happen in Lhasa,' Mrs Wong said cheerfully. 'Please, Miss Copleigh, don't be afraid. Okay?'

'Silly Madge,' Seton said softly, brushing the curls away from her forehead. His eyes were tender, amused. 'It's just the altitude. I've been seeing monks all morning.'

'But he was so *real*,' Madge protested, staring up into his face with wide green eyes. 'He even smiled at me!'

'When I first came to Lhasa,' Mrs Wong volunteered, 'I once saw a whole procession of monks, in their high red hats, beating cymbals and drums. They weren't there. It's just the effect of oxygen starvation.'

'I think you'd better get back to that oxygen cylinder in our bedroom,' Seton smiled. Madge closed her eyes as he kissed her on the mouth, his lips warm and firm.

'An excellent idea,' the guide nodded, her eyes soft as she watched them. 'It's lunchtime, after all, and I've kept you far too long. You'll feel much better after a meal—and then you can start making your film. Okay?'

'Okay,' Seton smiled. 'And it's been a most fascinating tour, madame. We're in your debt.'

Mrs Wong beamed her pleasure. She was obviously far from immune to Seton's male charm. 'So—we go out this way.'

They followed her neatly-trousered figure down the dark hallway.

Madge leaned blissfully against Seton's supporting arm, so strong around her waist. It had been worth that moment of sheer terror to see the tenderness in his eyes, to taste the sweetness of that kiss!

For the first time in nearly twenty-four hours, life didn't seem utterly bleak to her.

CHAPTER SIX

AFTER two days of intensive filming, they had built up a good picture of the Potala. They had covered most of the important objects and chambers in the palace—though they hadn't managed to capture any of the ghostly monks which they both still saw now and then—and they had recorded a fascinating interview with one of the head Lamas, a saintly old man not unlike the monk of Madge's vision.

Working with Seton had been a revelation to Madge. Thinking back on her earlier hostility and touchiness, she had been ashamed. This man was a master of his craft, a genius both with cameras and with people; he had coaxed the head Lama into one of the most touching and spiritual conversations she had ever witnessed, describing with utter frankness his faith, his inner experiences, his life under the Chinese administration. On screen, she knew that this interview, edited down to twelve minutes of broadcast time, was going to be brilliantly effective. Something unique in Western television history. So were the scenes of the great halls, all shot in the eerie natural light available there. That had been Madge's special province, and she had been working with all the meticulous care she could muster, determined not to let Seton down—or incur anything but praise.

At this point, though, their film still needed something to hold it together, some unifying factor that would make it a piece of cinema as well as a factual documentary. It was something that was becoming more urgent now that they were nearly finished the basic shooting-script Seton had worked out months back.

'Did you notice,' Seton asked thoughtfully over dinner, 'the tomb of the Sixth Dalai Lama?'

'I don't think so.' She glanced up enquiringly from the exotic lotus-root omelette the chef had prepared for them. She had been slightly more at ease with Seton since her monk-hallucination, and now that work had started in earnest; even sharing a room, though presenting occasional embarrassments, hadn't been too fraught. 'Why? Was it particularly beautiful?'

'No. It wasn't there.'

She searched his face, wondering what was in his mind. 'Where is it, then?'

'Nobody knows.' He smiled briefly. 'The Sixth Dalai Lama fell into disgrace for his worldly ways, and was expelled from Lhasa. They say he died as a goatherd in Outer Mongolia.'

'Is that important?'

'As important as a Pope being kicked out of Rome for having a dozen mistresses.' He drained his glass of bitter Chinese beer, and leaned back with hooded eyes. Madge studied him, her face cupped in her hands. He managed to make even the simplest clothes look stunning; the black jeans he wore hugged the sleek muscles of his hips and thighs, and the thick ribbed sweater he had put on against the Lhasa cold emphasised the supple power of his torso.

'Who *was* the Sixth Dalai Lama?' she asked, trying to keep her mind from wandering into forbidden regions.

'His name was Tsangyang Gyatso. He was the one who built that pagoda on the lake in front of the Potala. That was a hideaway for his mistress. He's said to have spent more time in her arms than meditating on the scriptures. Also, he frequently got drunk on *chang*, and was a good customer at the local House of Joy.'

'You're joking!'

'I'm not.' He stood up. 'Let's take a walk outside.' They waved to Mrs Wong, who was eating with a group of Chinese officials at a nearby table, and strolled out into the Tibetan night. It was cold, but in this far northern latitude the night sky was light, and misty with stars. 'Tsangyang Gyatso was no libertine,' Seton went on as they strolled into the garden. 'He was a sensitive man who wrote beautiful love-poems to his woman, full of anguish and longing.'

'But how did a man like that get to be Dalai Lama?' she asked in puzzlement. They sat on a low stone wall, and she stared up at the looming shape of the Potala, dominating the city. 'There must have been some kind of a mistake.'

'Yes. The Dalai Lamas are all supposed to be reincarnations of the Buddha. They aren't elected—they're discovered. At the moment the Dalai Lama dies, his new incarnation is believed to be born somewhere in Tibet—and the Lamas go in search of him.' She listened in fascination to the velvety voice beside her. It was a voice you just sank into, she thought, a voice that wrapped itself around you ... She shivered, longing for the warmth of his arms, and tried to concentrate.

'But how do they know which baby is the right one?'

'There are various signs—marks on the body, the shape of the skull and ears, a whole array of tests.' He brushed her cheek with warm knuckles. 'Are you cold?'

'No.' Her skin tingled at his touch. 'So they got it wrong with the Sixth Dalai Lama?'

'In a way. For one reason or another, Tsangyang Gyatso was a grown boy by the time they'd found him. Normally, the baby Dalai Lama would be brought up in the Potala, trained for his life as god-king. Tsangyang Gyatso's character was already formed—and he found himself thrust into a greatness he didn't want. He was obviously a sensual man, a man who loved making love, touching the woman he adored. That's obvious from his poems. Yet he was forced into an existence where the flesh was forbidden. He wanted nothing more than to taste sweet wine with his mistress—yet he found himself the spiritual leader of a whole nation, who expected him to behave like a saint. He seems to have done his best, but he just couldn't take it. He used to slip out of the Potala and roam around Lhasa, getting drunk and generally painting the place red.

'The end came when he fell in love—really in love— with a blue-eyed woman. She was the one he wrote all those love-poems for. Tsangyang became obsessed by her. He built the Serpent House, the pagoda in the lake, for her, and they made a kind of love-nest there. But she finally fell pregnant, and had his child—and that was that. The Lamas sat in council, the girl and the baby were killed, and Tsangyang was spirited off into exile, where nobody really knows what miserable end he came to.'

'That's sad,' she said slowly, 'very sad. I guess the Lamas were furious with him?'

'Yes. They did their best to wean him away from all these forbidden delights,' Seton said, also glancing up at the mass of the Potala above them. 'They initiated him into secret sexual tantras to try and keep his mind off his beloved—but that didn't work.'

'Tantras?' she queried.

'Rituals,' he replied. 'The Tibetan Buddhists believe that many forms of lovemaking exist, spiritual as well as physical. They say that a man and a woman can make love with their minds and souls.' He glanced at her. 'Without need of their bodies.'

'Is that true?' she asked, wishing she could see into those midnight-blue eyes.

'That they believe it—or that it works?'

'Well—both.'

'These tantric practices have been known for centuries,' he shrugged. 'Some of them even involve the partners physically making love. But at the higher levels, only their minds make contact. It's still a sexual interchange, but it's their spirits which meet, touch, become one.'

'But is that possible?' she asked, fascinated.

'Lots of lovers who aren't Buddhists have that sort of experience,' he said gently. Madge chewed her lip for a second. Had Seton and Lana ever been that close? she wondered. And found herself suddenly murderously jealous of a dead woman.

Ashamed of her own reaction, she asked, 'And it really—works?'

'It would certainly be interesting to try,' he said with a touch of dry amusement in his deep voice. 'But we were talking of Tsangyang Gyatso.'

'Sorry,' she said, suddenly awkward. 'What made you find out all that information about him?'

'Because it occurs to me that the Sixth Dalai Lama would make an interesting focus for this film. He kind of sums up the whole problem of Lamaism, the paradox of being a god-king. He reminds us of the human body under the saffron robe. Of the conflict within so many religious people—the struggle between desire and holiness. Tsangyang knew all about the tensions that exist in that palace on the hill. He knew what it was like to be a reluctant god.'

'A reluctant god,' Madge nodded slowly. And smiled slightly sadly to herself, thinking how appropriate that would be as a title for Seton. 'Yes, it's perfect.'

'Think of how he must have felt. He had everything in the world—immense power, prestige, wealth. The only thing he couldn't have was the one thing on earth he really wanted—love. That ties the whole thing together. Obviously, we can't make too much of Tsangyang, because very little is known about him. But somehow I find his story moving. And I think it'll throw a lot of light on Lamaism for the viewers.'

'Yes,' she said again, 'it is a moving story. And

you're right—it does cast a lot of light on Lamaism.'
She looked up at him, thinking that the story also cast a
lot of light on Seton himself. His powerful sympathy
with Tsangyang Gyatso poignantly suggested the strain
he himself was under, the need to keep his emotions
locked away, to deny himself the love she knew he
needed. 'Are you going to use the idea?' she asked.

'It's a joint decision,' he said matter-of-factly. 'We're
a team, Copleigh. What do *you* think?'

She sat in a surprised silence. So he had really meant
it when he'd said they would work together! A smile of
delight crossed her mouth in the darkness.

'I like the idea,' she said firmly, 'I think it'll work.'

'So do I.' He stood up, and smiled down at her in the
darkness. 'Let's get back inside and start working on
that script.'

She nodded, and feeling positively happy, walked
beside him into the bright lights of the Guest House.

It was only at the very end of the evening that Madge
finally found the courage to ask the question that had
been buzzing in her mind all night. She had bathed
luxuriously after a hard three or four hours' work
together, and had wrapped her slender body in her
dressing-gown for decency's sake as they prepared for
bed. Brushing her hair into burnished copper at the
mirror, she watched Seton from under her thick lashes
as he filed away the mass of notes and directions they
had decided on for the next day's shooting.

'Can I ask you something?' she blurted out.

'Go ahead,' he invited without looking up.

'This evening you said that some lovers get close
enough to each other to—to be able to make love with
their minds as well as their bodies.'

His eyes jolted hers in the mirror.

'Well?' he prompted grimly. She turned in her chair
to look at him, her smooth cheeks reddening.

'Were you and Lana as close as that—ever?'

His brows came down, ominous as thunderclouds, and he rose to toss the files on to their writing-table. 'That's a very personal question.'

'You don't have to answer it,' she said quietly, dreading his anger and yet unable to resist her need to know.

'Thanks,' he replied with silky irony—and turned his broad back on her, hauling off his sweater. Madge bit her lip in the tense silence that followed. Another statuesque snub for Copleigh.

But to her surprise, he went on.

'What the hell makes you think you've got the right to ask questions like that, anyway?'

'I don't think I've got the right.' She watched him unbutton the bush-shirt he wore. 'I just thought we were becoming friends.'

'Friends?' he repeated, turning to lift a scornful eyebrow at her. She dropped her lashes over hurt green eyes.

'I said you didn't have to answer.'

Seton sighed explosively, and pulled off his shirt. 'You're a funny kid, Copleigh. You say the damnedest things.' In silence, she watched the sinewy power of his naked chest, then looked away. 'Can't you see that it isn't easy for me to talk about Lana?' he growled. He sat on the bed, leaning back on his elbows to study her with electric blue eyes. 'It isn't easy to just look back and say "It was like this, or this". Sometimes it hurts.'

'That's the first time you've ever admitted a human emotion in my presence,' she said, meeting his eyes with a touch of defiance.

'Is that really how you see me?' he rejoined. 'Callous, inhuman?'

'Not any more,' she admitted with a quick smile. His stomach muscles were in clean, perfect relief, the crisp dark hair adding mystery to his golden skin. 'I'm beginning to feel you might be human after all. You've even called me "Madge" a few times.'

'"Madge",' he grimaced. 'Are things like that really so important to you?'

'No woman likes to be called by her surname,' she said, her expression still defiant. 'It's de-humanising. According to the grapevine, you get around with plenty of women. I'll bet you don't call them by their surnames.'

'There's too much gossip at Studio Seven,' he growled. His eyes dropped to her breasts. The dressing-gown had fallen open slightly, and the creamy swell of one shapely breast was visible, ambiguously inviting. She drew the gown closed hastily.

'So you call them all Jones or Smith or whatever? Even in the most intimate moments?'

'There's a subtle distinction,' he said drily, 'between lovers and colleagues.'

'So you admit you have lovers?' she flashed, her eyes angry.

'What is this?' he snapped back. 'A marital tiff? We're on a job here, Copleigh, not a blasted honeymoon. And my love-life is none of your goddamned business!'

'Watch your goddamned language!' she retorted, and spun back to face her own sparkling gaze in the mirror, using the hairbrush as though it were a weapon to punish her own folly in trying to get any closer to this rhinoceros-skinned man.

Lying in the dark, later, Madge couldn't relax. It was hard to be calm with the knowledge that Seton was only a few feet away, probably as wide awake as she. Why was it that they only managed to get along on a purely business basis? And why couldn't she resist Seton's fatal magnetism over her?

Every time she made the slightest move to get closer to him, they just ended up hating each other. Maybe, she thought wryly, we're opposite poles. As soon as we get too close, we repel each other, whether we want to or not.

She rolled on to the side facing him, and stared into the darkness with troubled eyes.

His voice reached out to her, soft, husky.

'Of course we were close. When I married Lana, we were in love. Do you know what that feels like?'

'No,' she said in a small voice.

'I'm afraid I can't explain it, then,' he said grimly. 'But that's the way it was eight years ago. Lana and I were young. Life was wonderful, we were wonderful, everything was wonderful. And if you really have to know, sex was pretty wonderful too.'

'I see,' she whispered, a sharp pain making her want to curl up in sheer misery.

'That was in the beginning,' he said bitterly. 'It didn't last much longer than any other summer flower. I scarcely knew Lana when I married her. I just thought I was doing the right thing, trusted in Providence to make us wise and happy. And I thought Lana was the most wonderful thing that had ever happened to me. I didn't know about the ghosts and delusions in her head, or the weakness inside that destroyed her. It all went rotten very soon. And the sex went rotten first of everything.' She heard him turn restlessly in the bed. 'Does that answer your question?' he rasped.

'Yes,' she whispered.

'I'm glad to hear it.' She lay in silence, his bitter words echoing in her head. 'What made you ask that in the first place?' he asked, his voice gentler.

'Nothing. Just curiosity.'

'You puzzle me,' he sighed. 'I don't think I've ever met someone quite like you.'

'Oh?' Madge smiled tightly in the darkness. 'What makes you say that?'

'You're a strange mixture of things. Sometimes you behave like a teenager, other times you're mature, calm. Sometimes you're a woman, sometimes a child. I never know which person I'm going to meet next.'

She blinked in surprise. 'I've been having problems working you out as well,' she said slowly. 'I didn't realise it was mutual.'

'Which are you?' he asked. 'Woman or child?'

'I think of myself as a woman, Seton,' she replied gently. 'Maybe that's over-optimistic.'

'No. Sometimes you *are* a woman. Disturbing and infuriating—but definitely a woman.' She heard the smile in his voice. 'Other times you're a sulky, petulant girl.' He paused. 'Are you a virgin, Copleigh?'

Her mouth tightened, and she closed her eyes.

'No,' she said, her voice strained.

'Why sound so ashamed?' he said drily. 'I get the impression that it's a distinctly unfashionable thing to be these days.'

'I don't think fashion has anything to do with it!' she snapped sharply.

'Well, well,' he said wonderingly, 'I seem to have touched on a painful area. Haven't your affairs been very happy?'

'There was only one *affair*, if you want to call it that,' she grated. 'And it was a long time ago.'

'Indeed,' he mused. 'Care to tell me about it, seeing as we're in the mood for heart-to-hearts tonight?'

'I doubt whether my boring little mistakes will hold your interest very long,' she said sourly.

'You could try,' he said casually. 'What was your mistake's name?'

'His name was Andrew,' she said, rolling on to her back, and staring into the unravelling film-clips of her mind. 'Andrew Everett, my partner in crime.'

'Is sex a crime?' Seton asked gently.

'Running away with an under-age girl for immoral purposes is a crime in California,' she replied with humourless irony. 'We both seem to have met our Nemesis in Los Angeles, don't we? I know all about those Californian summers, Seton. We were even there around the same time. Maybe we even passed on Sunset Boulevard, who knows? And I also know about the optimism of youth. And the stupidity.'

'So it seems,' he said calmly. 'You ran away from home with this boy?'

'If I'd had a home to run from,' she nodded. 'All I ran away from was a house. A big, beautiful, empty house.'

'Your mother's?'

'My father's. That was eighteen months after the divorce. The divorce was big news, you know.' Her mouth was tight as she thought back to those terrible months of nakedness and pain. 'It was a long battle, and somehow two rival film companies got into the act as well, one on each side. It was in the papers every weekend—everything. All the affairs they'd both had, the terrible things they accused each other of having done, the weapons they'd used to try and destroy each other. And I was one of the main weapons they had.'

'So you turned and ran?'

'No. That came later.' She smiled without amusement. 'The court settled that I had to spend six months a year with each of my parents. But the crazy thing was that neither of them really wanted me in the first place. My parents are allergic to responsibility, Seton. They always will be. The wrangle over getting custody of me was purely for publicity.'

'That sounds a harsh thing to say,' he said softly.

'Maybe,' she shrugged painfully. 'It's the way I felt then. Because I knew I was just in the way when I went to stay with either of them. I might as well have not been there. My mother scarcely had the time to sit down to a meal with me. And she was always in hotels, which meant that for six months of the year I was following her around from hotel to hotel, never getting any proper schooling or making any proper friends.' She took a deep breath. 'I hardly saw my dad. He's got this mansion in Los Angeles that used to belong to Clark Gable for a while—but I was practically on my own there. He was always with women, always drinking or gambling or working or all three. I was supposed to be going to the local convent school—can you imagine? A convent school! The nuns used to treat me like the Scarlet Whore of Babylon. They only took me on because my father built them a new swimming-pool. Anyway, I just stopped going in the end. There was no one at home to check up on me, only the maids—and they didn't give a damn. So I just ran wild. In a desolate sort of way.'

'I understand,' Seton said in a gentle voice.

'Andrew came from Santa Monica,' she went on, the words flooding out of her as they hadn't done in her life before. 'We met on the beach one day, and just got talking. Andrew said we should just leave together, leave the whole crazy set-up and never come back. He had problems of his own, a father in jail for embezzlement and a mother who was off on drugs or Martinis half the time. We formed the kind of friendship that lonely kids form. Does all this sound terribly self-pitying to you?'

'No. Go on.'

'We only knew each other for three months. That's how silly it was. Andy had a car, a huge Chevy Impala with air-conditioning and a stereo system, and we used to go for long drives in it. Miles and miles in the summer sun, just talking and laughing and bitching about our parents, puffing cigarettes clumsily. And when he said one day that we should just keep driving, get married somewhere far away, and start our own lives, I thought—*why the hell not?*'

'You were in love with Andy?'

'I was seventeen,' she smiled wryly. 'Who knows what's in a seventeen-year-old's heart?'

She heard him climb out of bed and pad over to the

cupboard. 'There's a bottle of whisky in here somewhere,' he said. 'Want a drink?'

'Yes, please,' she said without hesitation.

He splashed whisky into two glasses, then pulled the heavy curtains open. The pale night sky was full of stars, and his body was silhouetted against the window for a moment before he brought the glass over to her. She took it, sitting up. The warm smell of his skin brushed her face, and her pulses jumped. Suddenly shy, she looked away, clutching the glass in both hands—and was distinctly relieved when he slid his dressing-gown over his shoulders.

'To the Sixth Dalai Lama,' he said ironically. Madge sipped the fiery liquor, relishing the way it seemed to burn away the remembered pain, cauterising the old ache.

Seton lay back on his own bed, the starlight touching the naked skin of his chest and the harsh lines of his face. A pool of darkness hid the rest of his body, making him mysterious, somehow unapproachable.

'So,' he prompted quietly. 'You took off with Andrew.'

'We only got as far as San José,' she said, tearing her eyes away from him. 'We ran out of gas. Can you believe it?'

'I can believe it.'

'We stayed in a motel,' she said, her mouth turning down with amused disgust. 'I guess we'd learned that kind of thing from our parents. It was called the Eezy Q. Ranch, a mile or two out of San José, just off the highway. We could hear the cars all night. You could see their headlights move across the ceiling.' She cradled the glass in her hand and leaned her cheek against its cool side, remembering. 'We holed up there for three nights, me and Andrew.'

'And you slept together?' he asked quietly.

'We were going to get married,' she said in a dry

voice. 'It seemed like the natural thing to do. So I gave up my virginity to Andy.' The words came out as brittle as she felt, as ashamed and bitter. 'In the Eezy-Q. Ranch Motel, two miles out of San José. Over three humid summer nights.'

'Don't sound so cynical,' he smiled. 'There are less romantic ways of losing your virginity, believe me.' He looked at her in the darkness. 'And that was your first and last experience with the lusts of the flesh?'

'Yes.' She had told the story as unemotionally as she could, leaving out the ugly details. The greed with which Andy had approached her body, the utter lack of affection in his hands and mouth. The way she had felt polluted by the contact. The clinging sense of shame. The obsessive way she had showered after they had slept together, as though to scrub his very touch from her skin. The way she had cried almost all the time. The way Andy had failed, the way she had had to commiserate with him over his sexual inadequacies and shortcomings, even when her own soul was sick with nausea and regret.

No, it hadn't been an experience she had ever wanted to repeat. She had never told the whole story to anyone, had never wanted to relive the depression and the sordidness. But Seton had made it easy for her, as though in some profound way he understood. And she hadn't just been telling him the story. The very depth of her attraction to Seton had forced her to review that long-past relationship in the most fundamental way; and despite the pain, she had been able for the first time to see her experience with Andy as a mature woman, not as a tormented adolescent. And that had been a unique, somehow cleansing experience.

Feeling a lot better, she gulped the liquor down and grimaced. 'God, I hate whisky!'

'And making love? Did you enjoy that?'

'I'm afraid not,' she flushed. 'There wasn't any meeting of minds or souls, if that's what you mean.

Andy claimed to know a hell of a lot about sex—all Californian kids do. But I wasn't expecting much. And I wasn't wrong.' She paused, her flush deepening. 'To be frank, it just disgusted me.'

'Experience always hurts,' Seton said sardonically. 'You've had no urge to repeat the experiment?'

'Not so far,' she said tersely. 'Andy was—I don't know how to put it—*greedy*. I felt defiled.'

'It doesn't always have to be like that,' he said mildly.

'I have no proof of that,' she said with a touch of asperity. 'After Andy, I swore I'd never get into anything like that situation again, ever.'

'Very moral,' he said silkily.

'Sneer if you like,' she retorted. 'I don't pretend to be virtuous—just cautious.'

'That's an aphorism I rather like,' he smiled. 'How did this escapade end?'

'Andy's mother got the State Police out after us.' She winced at the memory of the bored, cold faces behind the obligatory sunglasses. 'They tracked Andy's car down in no time, and just picked us up.' She drew a shaky breath. 'That hit the headlines—especially as Andrew's mother claimed I was a teenage nymphet who'd seduced her son. Dad was furious with me! And my mother got a court injunction to take me away from him. So—I went back to England, sadder and wiser. And minus my maidenhood.'

'And minus a few illusions, by the sound of it.' Seton drained his glass, a dark, pagan figure so near to her, and yet so distant. His eyes were dark, cryptic. 'Were you suitably chastened?'

'Oh, that was the end of my adolescence,' she said with a brittle laugh. 'For a long time I felt that I was exactly what they were calling me—a slut, a fallen woman. I really despised myself.'

'What changed that?' he asked, still watching her face in the starlight.

'You,' she smiled. 'Not you personally—your film. *The Whale's Song*. That film was—oh, it was a revelation to me. It was so full of mystery, so haunting. It showed me how much majesty there was in life, how much dignity and beauty.' She leaned back against the pillow, smiling dreamily. 'I'll never forget the evening I watched it. I just cried and cried. And from that moment, I knew I had a purpose in life, that there was something I wanted to do really badly. And that gave me myself back. It showed me that I could escape from the sort of life my parents were living, the sort of life I was heading for, and make my own decisions.' She looked at Seton's dark form. 'That's what changed me. Two months later I was eighteen. I managed to get a grant to go to film school, and I left home as soon as I could. Three years later I found myself working for the great Seton Chambers' studio.'

'A fairytale come true,' he said drily. Yet she sensed that he had been stirred by what she had said. 'So that's what you were trying to tell me, that day in the corridor?' he asked. 'And I just walked away!'

'I hope you're suitably repentant,' she said, her laugh sounding brittle. She paused. 'Do you despise me now?'

'Why should I despise you?' he asked in surprise.

'For having given my all to Andy Everett in the Eezy Q. Ranch Motel,' she said. She'd tried to sound jokey, but her desperate seriousness was audible, like a silent cry hanging in the air.

'No,' he said, and the soft roughness of his voice showed that he had heard that cry. 'I don't despise you. I feel really sorry that it had to happen to you that way. And I wish for your sake that it could have been different for you. But you're a fool to think I could despise you.'

'You can't wish things undone,' Madge said in a small voice. 'But sometimes I also wish it had gone differently. That it had happened with someone else.'

She closed her eyes, thinking, *maybe even someone like you*.

'Maybe losing your virginity seemed immensely important at the time,' he said with a smile in his voice. 'But it wasn't the end of the world. And from what you tell me, your escapade with Andy hardly counts. What really matters is the future, the life you've got ahead of you. The love you're going to have. Life doesn't always conform to our expectations of it, unfortunately,' he went on drily, 'but you've got so much going for you—beauty, talent, brains. You shouldn't be so unhappy about the past; it belongs to no one. But the future is yours.' He stood up and took her empty glass, and rinsed both glasses out at the basin.

He returned, and to her surprise, sat down beside her.

'Get back into bed,' he commanded, pulling the blankets aside. She obeyed dumbly. 'Take your gown off.' As she hesitated, he smiled. 'Don't worry—I can't see anything in this light. Just lie on your stomach and relax.'

She rested her cheek against the cool pillow, and Seton drew the sheets away from her shoulders, and began to rub her back lightly.

'Listen to me, Madge,' he said gently, his hands warm on her skin, 'because I'm not going to say this again. To you I may seem like some kind of machine, cold and unemotional. Well, that's exactly the way I want to seem. I learned long ago that there's no room on this sort of assignment for any ambiguity, any misunderstanding between film people. Understand?'

She nodded, her whole body relaxing languorously under the sensual spell of his palms. Unlike her own clumsy attempt, this was an expert massage, a delicious easing away of tension and worry.

'There's something else,' he went on, his fingers kneading the delicate muscles under her satiny skin. 'You've heard through the grapevine that I'm not exactly short of female company.' She nodded. 'I've never been tied to another woman, not since Lana. The only relationships I've wanted since Lana have been purely physical ones. No ties, no guilt, no complications. And preferably no emotion. Just mutual amusement.' His hands stopped for a moment, then resumed their slow caress of her naked back. He laughed harshly. 'I wouldn't recommend living like that to anyone else, but it works for me. The faculty of being able to trust another human being was burned out in me long ago, Madge. And because of that I couldn't ask any woman to trust me in return.'

'But——'

'The reason I'm telling you all these intimate details,' he interrupted, 'is that I happen to like you. A lot. And I sense that you're on the brink of getting a lot of silly ideas about me, despite all my warnings.' *On the brink?* She bit her lip hard. 'If you were one of the sort of women I usually meet, I might even consider it,' he said quietly. 'But you're not. They're experienced, they know how to protect themselves. You don't. You don't have that hardness in you, Madge—that basic amorality, if you like. With you it would be deeply emotional, full of ideas like permanence, commitment, responsibility. I can't give those things to anyone. Quite frankly, they terrify me. And I like you too much to hurt you that badly.'

Her eyelashes were wet, but she said nothing. As if sensing her pain, Seton leaned forward, and brushed the silky skin of her back with his lips.

'And don't think I'm not tempted,' he said huskily, 'because I am. And I always will be. If it's any consolation to you, no one has ever offered me the illusion of happiness the way you do.'

He laid the sheets back over her shoulders, and she heard him get into bed.

'Goodnight, Madge,' he said.

'Goodnight,' she mumbled, her heart aching.

The illusion of happiness . . .

How ironic! She would have given up her soul to make him happy, to show him that there was still a place in his life for love. Were it not for her own doubts. Maybe he was right. Maybe happiness *was* an illusion, like love, and trust, and passion. Illusions as immaterial and mutable as clouds.

She curled up into a ball, the memory of his touch lying like fire against her naked skin. She hadn't felt this rejected, this alone and in pain, since her adolescence. She, who had always played it so cool in her relationships with men, who had avoided physical or emotional contact like the plague! Who had made a mistake she had sworn never to repeat.

And who was now aching to be loved by a man she had once dismissed as the most unlikeable person she had ever known . . .

CHAPTER SEVEN

THE electricity had failed again the night before, and when Madge awoke in the morning, her room was redolent of the yak-butter lamp she had used to light herself to bed. The wind was still moaning outside the stone walls of the hut, and it was piercingly cold. Oh, for the Guest House at Lhasa! There it had been at least safe and comfortable. And Seton's warm body had been only a bed away.

But Lhasa was almost two weeks behind them now, and in this village house in the foothills of the Himalayas there had no longer been an excuse for her and Seton to share a room. Huddled in her sleeping-bag, she pulled the alarm clock closer. Eight-thirty. Seton would have been up for an hour already, and judging by the silence in the house, had probably driven into the village to check the weather over their last great objective—Kanchenjunga.

Stiffly she got out of bed, and walked to the window. The massive grandeur of the mountains never failed to take her breath away. They had seen so many exquisite things in Tibet—the treasures of the Potala and the massed gold of the Drepung monastery, which they had filmed next. They had spent two days in the Jokhang temple, where they had seen some of the most beautiful and precious Buddhas of all. The Summer Palace, strangely forlorn and deserted-looking, had been one of the most poignant parts of their tour.

There, more than anywhere else in Tibet, Madge had been aware of the inextricable mixture of sorrow and glory in this strange country. There, too, among the silent gardens and temples, she had been able to think clearly about herself and about Seton for the first time in days. There she had been able to come to some conclusions. Some of them had surprised her.

For example, there had been the old-style Tibetan wedding they had attended. She had started out with the impersonal interest of a photographer, intent on recording all the colourful detail of the ceremonial on film, but had found herself at first fascinated, then deeply emotionally caught up, in the beautiful ritual of the wedding. It suddenly hadn't mattered that the bride and groom were Tibetans, exotic and colourful—they were universal, this young couple, like any man and woman on the threshhold of married life. Until at the end she had found herself happily crying for the two of them and the innocent beauty of their hopes and faith in one another, as though she had known them both personally.

Afterwards, Seton had touched her wet cheeks thoughtfully, and had shaken his head.

'I'd have thought that you'd be the last person to get sentimental at a wedding, Madge—after what you've seen of your parents' marriage.'

'No,' she had smiled, drying her eyes, 'I've never been cynical about marriage, not even after Mum and Dad split up. I think it's the most beautiful and powerful of human relationships.' And it had been true. She had never thought of it before, but it was as though seeing her parents torment each other had only strengthened her faith in marriage as an institution. Seton had stared into her eyes for a few seconds, then had squeezed her shoulders hard, affectionately, and passed the matter off with a joke.

But that day had stayed in her mind for long afterwards, as a milestone in her understanding of herself, and what she wanted out of life. She knew that Seton himself had seen deeply into her soul through that incident. And she knew that what he had seen had

somehow kept him aloof from her ever since, as though
it had reminded him more emphatically than ever that
she wasn't the sort of woman he could have a casual
affair with.

Since then, they had travelled diagonally across Tibet
towards the great barrier of mountains in the south,
filming the everyday life of peasants and farmers,
exploring the life-style of this unique and far-flung people.

But nothing they had seen would ever come close, in
Madge's eyes, to the serenity and majesty of these
towering peaks—the mountains of Tibet, older by far
than any religion or political ideology. It had seemed
fitting to her that they were going to end their
documentary where they had begun—among the
striding giants of central Asia, the Himalayas.

She washed in the achingly cold water, the Chinese
soap lathering reluctantly on her fair skin with a faint
trace of sandalwood. Dressed in jeans, boots, and
heavy-duty anorak (it was going to be good to get back
to some feminine clothes!) she went into the tiny
kitchen, and started coffee.

The rather primitive little house had been rented to
them by the village commune, and it just about served
their needs. This concluding section of their film was as
unique in its way as the parts shot in Lhasa; the
Himalayas had seldom been filmed from the northern
side, and this incredible grandeur was as much a part of
Tibet as the monasteries or the Chinese-organised farm
communes.

The thing was that they had to get high enough
among the mountains to give their lenses enough scope
to capture it all—and the north face of Kanchenjunga
had seemed ideal. Except that when they had arrived,
an ominous haze had been hanging over the whole
Himalaya chain. Today the visibility was much better,
but that mightn't last even until the afternoon. And
they didn't have much more time . . .

Madge stared up at the peaks, naked and grand in the sunlight. How wonderful it must be actually to live up there! High above, nestling among the jagged peaks, was the Kanchen monastery, a grey fortress tipped with a gleam of gold. They had filmed it through their most powerful telescopic lenses yesterday, and Madge had marvelled at the human dedication that had hauled the materials up that precipitous cliffside centuries ago, and built a Buddhist monastery in the very heart of the Himalayas. Kanchen was the most remote, the most unchanged, of the Tibetan monasteries; they had been keen to film inside Kanchen as well, but the Abbot had firmly denied permission, saying that Kanchen had never been open to foreigners. Not even the Chinese administration, with its secular determination, had managed to penetrate those iron-grey walls! Kanchen, as Seton had put it, was going to keep its secrets for another few centuries yet.

Madge glanced through the door to where the cans of film stood in a bulky pile, covered in their protective wrappings. At least *they* would come to no harm in this piercing cold—film lasted much longer at low temperatures.

She smiled ruefully. Their precious film! Sum total of three weeks' intensive filming, stacked with Seton's characteristic attention to neatness and efficiency. She poured herself a cup of coffee, leaving the percolator half full for Seton, and sat down to drink the fragrant brew, her green eyes thoughtful on the cans of film.

She had learned a lot about Seton over these past fourteen days. After that night in Lhasa, she had thrust her half-formed romantic notions about him firmly back into their cage, and locked the door. It had been the only way for her to survive. Working with him had been almost incredibly tense for three or four days, then slowly their working relationship had re-established itself, and they had become the efficient camera team they were supposed to be, operating with cool respect for one another, smoothly and successfully.

And without pain? Maybe not. Some things hurt her, and would always hurt. One of them was that he never touched her, not even by accident. That squeeze at the wedding had been the last time their skins had made contact. Since then, that big, powerful body had maintained its self-sufficient distance from hers.

She rose, and stared out of the window at the little village that sprawled among the boulders and outcrops of rock below her. Not long now. Four days, and their visa was going to expire, and they would be back on that airliner from Katmandu to the world she had left behind.

Her world. Her mother, dripping publicity and pearls. Her father and his teenage girlfriends in California, slowly decaying in the too-hot sun. Melissa. Charlie.

Her career.

Suddenly depressed, she threw the dregs into the fireplace, and peered into the mirror to comb her hair. It had grown in these three weeks, glinting copper curls that now completely framed a heart-shaped face whose skin had been honey-tinted by exposure to the Tibetan sun through the thin air. Wide green eyes, made striking by thick, dark lashes. A neat nose. A full mouth, undeniably stubborn, haunted by a sensuality she had never really known what to do with.

Beautiful? Interesting, at least, to anyone who was looking. But she had given up expecting Seton to be looking. At the Summer Palace, in that peace, she had been able to get things into some kind of perspective. She had been able to recognise, at least, that her feelings for Seton went deep inside. And deep back into her past. She hadn't ever hated him; in fact, if she were honest, she'd been more than half in love with Seton Chambers ever since *The Whale's Song*. His stunning physical presence hadn't made things any easier. And in a crazy way, his icy indifference to her femininity had made him even more attractive to her, fascinated her more. The experience of that Tibetan wedding had served to emphasise the deep attraction, as well as the differences, that stood between them.

Maybe, she thought ironically, we women are as much hunters as men are supposed to be. Maybe like them, we're intrigued by the elusive, the rare.

Yet Seton was no longer a stranger to her, she thought, not any more. She picked up the battered light-meter he always carried on location. And she had learned a lot about the way he worked. Learned that he wasn't always the ice-man he seemed. He wasn't easy to read. She stared at the instrument with a faint smile. But there were hints she had learned to know him by. Like this light-meter, for example. She turned the meter in her hand, studying its scratched dial, the crack in the side which had been carefully glued together.

Things like this gave him away. Why did he carry this battered thing around? A man like him should have the best equipment, the most modern, the most efficient. This thing was fifteen years old. So why did she so often see it looped around his wrist?

Because you're sentimental, she thought. Just like me. Because you've had this a long time, and it reminds you of friends who aren't around any more, places you saw with younger eyes, other times and countries. She rubbed the smooth thing against her cheek, then dropped it back on to the couch with a grimace.

Damn Seton! Why did he always succeed in getting through to her, even when he wasn't there? Oh, Seton— I don't think I'm ever going to get over you. Not ever. And the only thing I've got to console myself with is a throwaway compliment I once heard in the dark—*don't think I'm not tempted. Because I am. And I always will be.*

It wasn't enough to tempt him. It wasn't enough to simply be desired. She needed more, needed his love. Needed to feel she belonged to him. That was what she had always wanted. *Nothing else has really mattered, has it?* she asked herself sadly. *You poor fool.*

The sound of the Land Rover's engine returning gave her sombre mood a glint of optimism.

There's one thing I know, at least, she thought firmly. *And that's the fact that your cool exterior is exactly as deceptive as the cool outside of an electric furnace!*

She braved the cold morning air to greet Seton as he climbed out of the Land Rover.

'Hi! There's hot coffee waiting.'

'Good.' He, too, had been bronzed by the high-altitude sun, his fiercely male face now almost the colour of a Tibetan's. Midnight blue eyes met hers with that old jolt, the old ache. 'You slept well?'

'Not bad.' She walked with him to the kitchen. 'I was cold, though.' *And I dreamed of you again* ... But she didn't say the words! He picked up his mug, but she took it firmly from him, and poured his coffee out, determined to be allowed to do *something* for him. He nodded his thanks, and gulped at the black, sugarless brew.

'I've been speaking to the chairman of the village,' Seton told her. 'He says Kanchenjunga's misting up again. He also says it'll stay that way for weeks.'

'Oh,' she said disappointedly. They had been waiting for Kanchenjunga's mood to lift for two days already, but despite brilliant sunshine, the slopes of mountains had been ghostly with mist, and Seton had refused to allow them to go up in such uncertain conditions. She had had to agree; on the drive from Nepal, she had seen time and again how mild mist could become a lethal fog or a violent snowstorm within an hour or two. They stared out at the picture-postcard mountain-scape beyond the village. There were veins of snow among the stone, spreading to form ice-berg caps of pure white along the peaks.

'It's so beautiful,' he murmured, almost to himself. 'I used to think that filming human violence was the way to change people's minds.' He turned to her with a wry smile. 'I started out as a photo-journalist, moving from war to war, trying to show people how senseless it all was, how sickening and futile. It didn't work.'

'Why not?' she asked in fascination.

'People just clapped, and said what good films they were. They weren't looking at the horror and the blood at all. They were just looking at the film, and thinking how well made it was. I realised that I was just helping people to forget the reality of conflict. And I was just getting sicker and sicker with it all.'

'How old were you then?' she asked.

'In my late twenties.' His smile became warmer. 'I wasn't very different from the way you are now—full of high ideals and principles. I was out to change the world.'

'And now?'

He laughed. 'I guess I'm still the same fool somewhere deep inside. But I don't try and show people the futility of war any more. It suddenly occurred to me that people had been trying to do exactly the same thing for centuries, with the same lack of success.'

'So you turned to wildlife films,' she guessed, watching his face. He nodded. 'To try and do the same thing in another way,' she went on quietly, realising that he was talking about something deeply important to him, something that came from deep inside.

'Yes,' he nodded, turning back to the window. 'I got caught up in a bad guerilla battle in the Middle East while I was on an assignment for one of the television companies. I was wounded, and all my equipment got blown up in somebody else's jeep.' Madge held her breath, utterly spellbound by this calmly-told story, by the image of Seton's violent past. 'I ended up being captured by the rebels. They treated me pretty roughly at first.' He shrugged. Madge's face was horrified, and he stroked her cheek gently. 'That's the way things were,' he smiled. 'It's all a long time back, now. When they realised I really was a journalist, we all became buddies. They took me up into the mountains with them, and I lived in a guerilla camp for six weeks.' He sighed softly. 'No shooting, no explosions, no bloodshed. Just peace, and the mountains. That was when nature started really meaning something to me. It was a kind of change inside me, that went on for a couple of years after that. The whole thing finally crystallised after Lana died. I realised that what I should really be doing was showing people how wonderful the world could be. How beautiful life really was. Trying to persuade them to stop the hate and the violence that way.' He smiled with a hint of self-mockery. 'Whether it works or not, I wouldn't like to say.'

'It worked for me,' Madge told him, holding his gaze with serious green eyes. 'It works, Seton.'

'I'm glad to hear it,' he said. It was impossible for her to tell whether he meant the smile or not—he was so good at hiding his real feelings behind some disguise. 'Well,' he said brusquely, 'that's enough about what a saint I'd like to be. Let's get back to this mountain. To climb or not to climb?'

It was an effort for her to tear her mind away from what he had been saying, and return to the urgent present. 'What do you think?' she asked.

'Today's the best day so far,' Seton said thoughtfully. 'At least it's bright enough to film.' He drained his cup. 'The question is—will we be able to get down again once we're up?'

'If we set off right now,' she suggested, watching his face, 'we could at least get some filming in before late afternoon. Then, if it starts turning nasty, we could make a run for it back to the village.'

'Yes,' he nodded. 'That thought had occurred to me as well. Our only other alternative is to scrap the mountain section of the film altogether, and fill it out with more footage of Lhasa and the temples.'

'No,' she said instinctively. 'The mountain section's too important. To me, it's the most important part of all.'

Seton smiled slightly, blue eyes warming for a second. 'I agree. Then you think the risk is worth it?'

'I trust you,' she said simply. Then, dropping her eyes from his, she smiled. 'Besides, if the worst comes to the worst we could always take shelter in Kanchen monastery.' He glanced up at the distant fortress, inaccessible miles up in the crags.

'That would be a unique way of getting inside,' he agreed. He hesitated, something she had almost never seen him do. 'Are you sure you want to take the risk, Copleigh? After all, it's only a film.'

'*Only a film?*' she repeated in mock-amazement. 'I never thought I'd hear you say those words! Yes, I'm sure.'

She watched him as he made up his mind. What he had told her about his earlier experiences had moved her profoundly, more than she cared to show him. It had also drawn her suddenly much closer to him. His idealism about war coincided exactly with her own revulsion towards violence in any form, and she could understand exactly the way he had felt then. She cringed at the thought of his being hurt, of that splendid body and mind being scarred by the senseless cruelty of other men. So that was how he had got those scars. She ached to be able to kiss them, to take away any pain that might still haunt him. Some day, she knew, she must ask him to tell her the whole story, leaving out nothing . . .

'Okay,' he said, making up his mind. 'But I'm going to pack the Land Rover with all our emergency gear—oxygen, survival blankets, iron rations, the lot. We'll go as far as we can by car, and then climb as high as we need to. With luck, we'll be able to get back before nightfall.' He strode to the neatly-piled boxes of their gear. 'That way we'll at least get some film of the Himalayas themselves. I agree that the film won't be complete without that.' His eyes glinted. 'Besides, it would be a great pity to waste all that training we did in London. Wouldn't it?' The reminder of her earlier stupidity and impertinence made Madge squirm uncomfortably as she joined him to help in packing the Land Rover.

'You must have thought me a complete idiot at first,' she said as she checked their oxygen cylinders.

'What makes you think I've changed my opinion?' he replied calmly, and carried an armful of supplies out into the cool morning sunlight, oblivious to her indignant expression.

At a thousand feet above the valley, two hours later, it was considerably colder, and the thin air had become so rarified that the Land Rover had begun to falter and struggle, its engine labouring to fire in the oxygen-poor atmosphere. The road, like the one they had come by from Katmandu, had been beaten over the centuries by camel and buffalo trains, and was savagely uneven in places. The snow which they had begun to encounter now was also making things difficult, disguising potholes and boulders in the path. But the valley below was a magnificent sight, a tapestry of dull greens and browns threaded with the turquoise lines of streams and rivers.

They had stopped once already to film the village, a child's toy far below them, and the magnificent panorama was growing ever more spectacular with each hundred feet they climbed.

'It's almost like a stormy sea,' Madge mused, clinging to the strap as the Land Rover jolted across the frozen track. 'A huge ocean whipped to a frenzy, then frozen into stone in a split second.'

'Give or take the odd split second,' Seton smiled, 'that's more or less what happened. This mountain range was forced out of the earth's surface over a couple of hundred million years by fantastically powerful contractions of the earth's crust as it cooled and solidified.' They both winced as the car jolted over deep ruts in the path. 'Four-wheel-drive doesn't beat four-leg-drive in this terrain,' he commented. 'Those pilgrims knew what they were doing when they took camels!' Another series of holes bounced the thin air out of their lungs.

'Look!' Madge called breathlessly, as they rounded a snowy bend in the track. The monastery of Kanchen was in view, three or four miles away. It was a starkly beautiful sight, rising massively out of the rock which seemed almost to have given it birth. Its forbidding fortress walls stared implacably on the valley below, spurning the sordid everyday preoccupations of humanity.

'Stunning,' Seton agreed. He pulled the car up, his tanned face alight with energy. 'Let's shoot that, and then take another long panning shot across the valley.' They clambered out, their breath condensing in white clouds. Now the cold really bit, and the air was thin enough to make Madge feel short of breath all the time. To their left, Kanchenjunga towered upwards. A steep slope studded with boulders and cracked ledges of rock loomed over them, and dropped sheer down into the valley far below to their right. They set up the tripod in the road, and Madge leaned against a boulder to watch Seton film. She felt strangely giddy up in this skyey world, almost as though she were continually falling. The altitude, she knew, would play such tricks on her.

Her eyes drifted from the fortress beyond to Seton's figure. His body was taut behind the camera, thighs braced as he swung the heavy machine slowly across and down to pan through the valley below. It was still misty, but not enough to do more than add a touch of mystery to their film. Madge prayed it would hold like that for a few hours at least.

She checked her watch.

'Twelve-thirty,' she called to Seton. 'How much higher do you want to go?'

He turned to her. 'High enough to be able to shoot the whole range.'

'Will the Land Rover make it much further?'

'I doubt it.' Effortlessly, he shouldered the big camera, and walked over to her. 'How are you feeling?'

'Great,' she lied. Seton slid the camera back into its place, then turned to her.

'You look pale, Copleigh.' He brushed the hair away from her forehead, the old gesture that brought back so many sharp memories. He took her wrist, his fingers warm against her cool skin, and felt her pulse. 'Fast,' he commented. 'And not very regular.'

'I'll be fine,' she repeated, pulling her hand away from his in embarrassment. His closeness, if he only knew it, was probably the main reason behind her rapid pulse! His expression remained unconvinced, his eyes watching her carefully from under heavy lashes. She still couldn't bear to be this close to him, or feel those eyes so intent on her. He had the power to make her whole body and soul shake. Abruptly, she turned away, not caring that she appeared brusque and mannerless, and hauled her camera out of the Land Rover. The slight effort seemed to exhaust her, but she covered the feeling, determined not to appear weak in front of him.

'If you want to climb, let's climb,' she said tersely.

He kept his eyes on her for a second, then shrugged. 'As you wish.' He stared up the mountainside, eyes narrowed against the pale light, then pointed to a jutting-out crag some four or five hundred feet up. 'We'll climb as far as there to start with, and see what the view's like.'

Madge's heart sank miserably. She thought of the way that school field had seemed to stretch interminably ahead, an impossible distance for wobbly legs and bursting lungs. Well, this was what she'd done all that training for. She shouldered her camera, and trudged up the track beside Seton.

The climb was gruelling, but not even the exhausting physical exertion seemed to bring Madge warmth. Her body felt cold right through, cold to the bone, and within a few yards of the start, the breath seemed to have gone from her lungs.

There was snow all around, the wind blowing deathly cold off it. The haze, though it had intensified, still wasn't an obstacle to filming; a haze filter, she knew, would enable their lenses to film perfectly through it. Above, the dome of the sky, a strange turquoise in colour, arched icily over this most fantastic of landscapes.

She had a strange sense of *déjà-vu* following Seton, her eyes dully fixed on his apparently tireless legs while her own body was ready to give up the fight. This was where the trip had begun—following Seton fruitlessly. In fact, she thought tiredly, she seemed to have been following Seton ever since she could remember, scrambling to keep pace with that powerful and indifferent body, ignored or at best barely tolerated . . .

He turned to look back at her. 'Okay?'

'Fine,' she nodded wearily, trying not to look as limp as she felt. He waited for her to come level with him, then looked carefully into her face.

'You're not fine at all,' he said grimly. 'You're dead on your feet.' His mouth hardened into anger. 'Why didn't you tell me you were so tired, you little idiot?'

'There's nothing wrong with me,' she retorted petulantly.

'The altitude—that's what's wrong with you,' he retorted. He took her face in his hands, and stared into her eyes. 'You look ready to drop,' he said more gently. 'You're not coming any higher with me.' He slid the camera off her aching shoulder and looped it over his own.

'But——'

'No buts.' He turned her firmly but gently, so that she was facing down the track. The Land Rover was a grey and white box far down below. 'Go back to the Land Rover, Madge.' He raised a warning finger as she opened her mouth to protest. 'Get inside, and wrap yourself in a blanket. Are you listening to me?' She nodded tiredly, not sure whether to be bitterly hurt or deeply relieved at his orders. 'And then have a mug of coffee from the Thermos flask. If you start feeling really cold, switch on the engine, and use the in-car heater. Okay?'

'Okay,' she muttered. She looked up at him with misty green eyes. 'I'm sorry, Seton.'

'Don't be silly.' And this time the smile was real, a gentle, affectionate smile that warmed her as instantly as hot brandy. 'You've done wonders. Now go—I'll be back within an hour and a half, no more.' Impulsively, she took the soft material of his anorak in her fists, and tried vainly to shake him.

'You be careful up there,' she said fiercely. 'You hear me?'

'I hear you.' He kissed her firmly on the lips, erasing the obstinate set her mouth had taken, pointed her in the Land Rover's direction, and gave her a gentle shove. 'Go easy on the way down.'

Feeling stupidly weak and weepy, she nodded, and began to stumble back down the way they had come. She didn't look back. She was too tired even to feel very elated at the affection he had shown her. Whenever he was worried about her, she had noticed, his mask dropped, and he couldn't keep back his feelings for her. Yes, she thought numbly, stumbling down the track, he *does* care about me. He does.

It was as dangerous descending as it had been climbing; the ruts in the track were inlaid with ice now, and whenever she stumbled, an alarming mini-landslide of rocks and pebbles erupted under her boots. She found time to pray that Seton would be safe in this lethally treacherous terrain. *Only a film.* She smiled weakly to herself. Seton would have climbed fearlessly into hell itself to get the film he wanted . . .

Madge's legs were trembling by the time she got to the car. Seton was little more than a blue speck high above her, and she had no way of telling whether he responded to, or even saw, her frantic arm signals. Tiredness seemed to have affected her eyes, making it difficult for her to see very far. She watched until he disappeared round a savage outcrop of stone, then hauled herself into the Land Rover's welcoming shelter. Obedient to Seton's instructions, she wrapped a blanket around her shivering body, and gratefully gulped down a mug of coffee. Nothing seemed to be really hot at this altitude; liquids boiled at a far lower temperature than at more reasonable altitudes, which somehow took the edge off her pleasure in coffee, a life-long addiction of hers. But the drink was life-restoring nonetheless. Warmth slowly made its way along her frozen veins.

Tiredness swept over her, and she curled up in her seat, pillowed her coppery head against one arm, and drifted into a dreamless sleep.

She was awoken by the drumming of rain on the roof. Stupid with sleep, she at first thought she was back in the house at the village. Then alarm jolted her into full wakefulness, and she sat up, clutching her blanket, and stared with dismay around. The turquoise clarity of the sky had given way to masses of dark cloud, sweeping down the mountainside just above the Land Rover, and bringing torrents of rain to lash at the naked mountains.

'Damn,' she whispered. Seton would be up there, in the midst of that swirl of cloud, defenceless. She looked at her watch. Carelessly, she hadn't checked the exact time they had parted—but it was three o'clock already, and she guessed Seton would have started back down by now.

The torrential rain whipped around the car in a sudden venomous rage, shutting Madge off from the outside world completely. The worm of fear twisted in her stomach. She'd be safe here—but Seton! He would be totally unprotected—and she had already had a taste of how quickly body heat could be drained away in this high cold; the danger of hypothermia suddenly became acutely real to her. And all their safety equipment was in the Land Rover.

It would be useless her trying to climb up to him with any of the gear. She simply wouldn't make it. But the Land Rover——

She stared at the wheel with frightened green eyes. Would she be able to get the Land Rover up that track? She'd driven four-wheel-drive vehicles before, but Seton had done all the driving in Tibet so far. She was out of practice, and a torrential downpour on Kanchenjunga wasn't the best place to start re-learning. But the car would certainly be able to climb where she herself couldn't.

And there really wasn't much choice. If she didn't get to Seton with the car, he might well get lost in that whirling rain, and lose his life to the mountain cold, as so many thousands had done before. The thought of Seton's danger galvanised her into activity. Tossing the blanket into the back, she scrambled into the driver's

seat and started up the engine. Its roar helped to give
her courage. She selected the lowest possible gear, and
cautiously let out the clutch. The wheels spun unevenly
in the mud, then the car lurched forward and began to
climb. Her heart in her mouth, Madge switched on the
headlights and concentrated on not letting the car lose
its grip on the ancient road.

The rain was still pouring down with a volume and a
sense of malice she had never experienced before.
Where in God's name had all this come from? The
track was only visible a few yards ahead of the bonnet,
and the double-speed wipers were losing the battle with
the rivers that cascaded down the windscreen, masking
the view ahead even more. Her heart rushed out to
Seton, alone and unsheltered in this elemental fury. She
risked second gear, but the big wheels immediately
started slithering among the loose stones and mud, and
she slammed the gearstick back, bouncing in her seat as
the chassis bucked across the ruts.

The track itself was fast becoming a rapidly-flowing
stream, and ferocious thumps from under the Land
Rover spoke of loose boulders that had begun to roll
down from above.

Where are you, my love? she agonised silently, her
eyes straining to pierce the terrible weather ahead. She
was in the cloud already, a maelstrom of rain and fog
all around her. Suddenly, nothingness loomed in front
of her, and she wrenched the wheel frantically to keep
the car from tumbling over the edge and down into the
valley a thousand feet below. The wheels somehow
clawed their way back on to the track, but from here on
the path was forbiddingly steep. Rain lashed down on
the car as she pressed the gas pedal flat on to the
boards, willing the Land Rover to climb, and not to
falter.

Obediently, it surged up the track, at such a steep
angle that Madge had a terrified thought it might

topple backwards and fall on to its roof. But it didn't.
She made it to the almost level spot where the rock
jutted outwards, and where she had last seen Seton.
Leaving the engine running, she jumped out and called
his name into the driving cloud.

Icy rain lashed painfully at her, drenching her in
seconds. And only the howl of the wind answered.
Madge fought down the panic in her mind. He had to
be up here somewhere, maybe within a few hundred
yards. She climbed back into the driving seat, oblivious
to her drenched clothes and hair, and leaned on the
horn for three minutes solid. The sound was oddly
tragic and desolate among the crags, and she guessed
that the wind might whip the sound away, mingling it
with its own weird moan, long before it reached Seton's
ears. Exhausted, but tense with anticipation, she waited
for any sign that he had heard.

None came.

She slammed the car into gear, and set off again into
the driving wall of mist. Again she found herself on the
very edge of the path, the wheels spinning jerkily among
the loose scree. She fought the car back, and swung in,
close to the shelter of the mountain. And then the track
was crumbling underneath the Land Rover, and it tilted
sharply sideways. Grimly, Madge trod the accelerator
on to the boards.

But this time it didn't help. The heavy vehicle was
moving inexorably sideways, two or more of its wheels
at a time whirling uselessly among the cascading gravel.
She spun the wheel as hard as she could, but the only
result was that the back of the car slid alarmingly
outwards, slewing the car sideways-on to the track. And
she was still moving backwards, the roaring engine
vainly trying to find somewhere to dig its heels in.

A savage noise was swelling around her, a growing
roar that numbed her terrified mind. It was coming not
from the engine, but from the mountain itself. The rock

beneath the Land Rover, loosened by centuries of rain and ice, was giving way. And like some creature stranded on an iceberg, the car—with Madge inside—was being carried over the edge of the cliff. She wrenched at the door, but it was too late. Among a swelling avalanche of rock and snow, the Land Rover slammed off the track, and toppled on to its side. Still slithering downwards, it spun on its axis among boulders that were almost its own size. The terrible jolting and clattering became a paroxysm, and Madge screamed as a massive stone smashed through the side window, adding diamonds of shattered glass to the debris cascading around inside the Land Rover. She covered her head and face with her arms, curling up against the door—which had become the floor. A giant fist slammed into her back, and she arched in winded agony, praying that the terror would stop. As she rolled helplessly sideways, something stabbed into the flesh of her inner thigh, making her scream. Then all the windows exploded into diamonds as the tumbling vehicle's frame was twisted by huge pressures. The car jolted on to its roof, and smashed, upside down, into a gulley a dozen feet below, accompanied by several tons of loose rock. The landslide continued for almost a minute more, some of the jagged boulders slamming with brutal force into the crippled car.

Slowly, the avalanche became a trickle, then dribbled to a halt. In the appalled silence, the rain swept down vengefully across the long scar in the mountainside.

CHAPTER EIGHT

CONSCIOUSNESS came with pain and fear. And movement. Thinking she was still falling, Madge screamed and reached out panic-stricken hands to grasp some support.

Or thought she did. In fact, little more than a murmur came out of her lips, and her hands stirred feebly against the warm body that was supporting her. Everything else was ice-cold. Only the body she lay against was warm.

Numbly, she tried to make sense of her position. She was being carried, she knew that, the way her father had sometimes carried her as a child, when she had been half asleep. Her head lolled against a broad shoulder, her right arm curled round a strong neck. Her left arm swung down his side, bumping against his thigh at each step he took.

Seton. The one overwhelming thought, that they were both alive, spread through her mind like a miracle. Then other things slowly became real. Bruises and sharp aches all over her body. Rain, still beating down on her cheek and sodden hair. Iron-hard arms supporting her, their fingers biting into her hip and shoulder.

'Seton . . .'

She found her face being carefully tilted upwards, and her eyes flickered open, blurred emeralds set in lids that were smudged with pain and exhaustion. It was evening. The sky above was dove-grey, the rain still washing down. And bitter cold. Lips kissed her brow, then her mouth. His face swam vaguely into view, its harsh masculinity softened by concern and compassion.

144

'Poor baby,' he said, the velvet voice gentle. 'How do you feel?'

'I don't know.' She tried a lopsided smile. 'Is this heaven?'

'You don't get a lot closer,' he said drily. With infinite tenderness, he wiped the curls off her cheeks and eyelids, where they had snaked wetly in the rain. 'Are you hurt?'

'All over,' Madge admitted. The golden blur of his face came into focus, and despite all her other pain, her stomach twisted at the concern in those dark eyes. Wonderingly, she reached up, and touched the passionate mouth with cold fingers. 'I didn't know whether you were alive or dead,' she whispered. 'I came looking for you——'

'You were a fool to do that,' he said. The harshness that had crossed his face eased slightly. 'A brave fool. It was only by the sheerest chance that I found the Land Rover. It was half buried in boulders.'

She shuddered. 'It was terrible... The whole mountain seemed to be falling on top of me. I thought I'd killed us both.' She tried to sit upright, but a surge of nausea and pain rose from nowhere, and Seton eased her back down as she retched helplessly.

'Take it easy,' he commanded.

'Where's the car?' she asked weakly, trying to fight down the sickness inside. The cold was making her shiver uncontrollably now.

'A long way back—about three miles. But it's totally wrecked, anyway. I had to tear the back doors off their hinges to get you out.'

'Three miles?' She tried to arrange her jumbled thoughts. 'Where are we, then?'

'About a mile and a half from Kanchen.'

'The monastery? Dear God, have you carried me all this way?'

'There wasn't all that much to carry,' he said drily.

'All that running around in Highbury seems to have done some good.' He lifted her with gentle hands, and she found herself staring up at the monastery, a dark fortress brooding over them about two kilometres away. '"Childe Roland to the Dark Tower came",' he commented.

'What are the monks going to say?' she asked apprehensively through chattering teeth.

'That remains to be seen,' he said with a slight smile. 'They're devout Buddhists, though, which ought to make them receptive to a couple of castaways.' He felt her pulse, watching her pale face. 'The sooner we get there the better, Madge. I'm going to lift you again, so brace yourself.'

'No!' she protested weakly. 'You've carried me far enough, Seton, God knows. You must be exhausted——'

'Do I look exhausted?' he asked, his expression forbidding.

'Yes,' she said sharply. 'You might be able to fool other people with that mask of yours, but not me. I've learned to know you too well.' She looked at the lines of strain around his eyes and at the corners of his mouth. 'And you're exhausted. Let me try and walk.'

'You've been out cold for the past hour or more,' he said quietly. 'You're almost certainly concussed. Apart from any broken bones you may be hiding. And you're shivering like a half-drowned dog.' Her mouth set into its most stubborn line, but he was unmoved. 'I doubt very much whether you could even walk across a carpeted floor—and the road to Kanchen isn't carpeted. The light's also failing. We could still quite easily die out here—especially if you choose this moment to start one of your tantrums.' Chilled by his words, Madge allowed him to lift her in his arms.

'Sorry,' she muttered against his hard shoulder. He didn't answer, and she wasn't sure if he'd even heard. Increasing consciousness was bringing more pains than she knew how to count. He was right—she would be totally unable to walk more than a few steps in her present shaken condition.

In fact, she thought bleakly, closing her eyes against the pain, she felt truly terrible.

And yet——

And yet she would have gone through it all again, just to see that look of compassion and concern in his eyes once more. She clung to him, feeling her love for him like a flame in the centre of her being, warming the ice and lighting the darkness. He had come for her, pulled her body from the crushed Land Rover, tenderly carried her in his arms across this wild mountainside. She smiled painfully against the broad shoulder under her cheek. It seemed that you had to get yourself half killed to extract any signs of caring from Seton. She drifted back into a semi-conscious dreamworld, her body becoming limp in his arms . . .

Gold and scarlet. Exquisite brocades of ancient silk and shimmering satin. A lacquered and inlaid chest of incomparable beauty. Madge fought down the sense of unreality that was beginning to swamp even the sharp aches of her bruised body. Her exhausted eyelids were closing of their own accord, despite the wonders of the room they were sitting in. She forced a smile as the wizened little Lama pressed a fourth cup of *tsampa* on her, and leaned against Seton as she stared at the thick, buttery concoction numbly.

'It'll do you good,' Seton told her quietly. 'Get it down.'

The three monks sitting opposite, their aged eyes full of concern and sympathy, nodded briskly, and made drinking motions. No one, so far, had been able to speak English, nor any of the languages she and Seton had tried them with; but the Lamas had been gentle and overwhelmingly hospitable.

But what were they waiting for?

The whole affair had taken on a crazy unreality, like a Mad Hatter's tea-party held in one of the great rooms at Versailles. This, by the look of it, was one of the monastery's reception chambers. They had been led here by the monk who had met them at the gate, his face as unperturbed as though such travelworn arrivals were commonplace at Kanchen. The room was even more lavishly comfortable than similar rooms they had seen at the Potala and the Drepung; the very carpets they sat on were Chinese silk, centuries old, and the walls were hung with gold and orange brocades, woven with an intricacy that was hypnotising Madge slightly.

Beside the low couch where she and Seton were sitting tiredly, a brazier burned brightly, its warmth adding to the heaviness which had been pressing on Madge's lids since they had been led up here almost an hour ago. She wondered what they looked like, two bedraggled Westerners sitting bleary-eyed among all this religious panoply.

The splendour certainly made a weird contrast with the worn brown robes the monks wore. Like the Lamas at the Drepung, these were mostly men in middle or late old age, their heads shaven, their wispy beards and drooping moustaches grey.

'I don't think they know what to do with us,' said Madge, resting her head against Seton's arm. 'Maybe they don't understand what's happened to us.'

'They understand,' he reassured her, supporting her wilting body with his arm around her waist. 'We're probably waiting for someone important to take a look at us—the Abbot or his deputy.' He arched his back painfully. 'God, I'm tired. You?'

Madge just nodded, snuggling against his arm like a tired puppy. The inquisitive stares of the Lamas didn't bother her any more.

Just then there was a stir of activity at the door, and

it opened to admit a Lama of around seventy, whose scarlet robe and arched hat proclaimed him to be someone of importance. Seton rose stiffly. 'This is the Abbot himself,' he guessed.

The old man hurried forward, his nut-brown face twisted in concern. He took Seton's hands in both his own, and tried a few rapid questions in Tibetan. They both shook their heads in incomprehension. The old man nodded, and studied them both carefully, asking with gestures whether they needed any medical attention. Madge shook her head with a weak smile, and pillowed her head on her clasped hands, pantomiming sleep.

The Abbot nodded briskly, and spoke rapidly to the waiting Lamas. Amid a general bustle, the two of them were beckoned to one of the doors. Madge clung to Seton as they followed the Abbot down a succession of long, dark corridors. The flickering yak-butter lamps cast dancing shadows, heightening Madge's dreamlike sense of unreality. Maybe, she thought wildly, I'm still lying in the Land Rover, hallucinating all this . . .

But the room they were led into was no hallucination. It was simply yet comfortably furnished with a huge bed, an enormous gilt sideboard, and a brazier that was burning warm and bright in one corner, illuminating the orange-painted walls. The impression of warmth and welcome was almost overwhelming, and for the first time Madge realised why oranges and reds were regarded as such sacred colours in this frozen land.

'Thank God!' she gasped, and sank down gratefully on to the featherdown comforter. She smiled blissfully at her hosts. There was a quiet murmur of leavetaking, and the Abbot gave them what was clearly a Buddhist blessing. Then the heavy wooden door closed, and they were alone together.

Seton sat beside her, his face at last beginning to show the strain and weariness of what he had been through. Without thinking, she melted against him, her arms holding him close.

'Thank you,' she whispered, 'for saving our lives.'

'Come on,' he said, smiling wearily, 'let's get some sleep.'

He unzipped her anorak, and pulled it off her shoulders. Too weak to do more than co-operate, she let him undress her, his fingers sure and gentle as they stripped off her cold, sodden clothes. Her jeans, especially, were filthy and torn, and the deep cut inside her left thigh had stained them with blood. It had begun to ache now, and she winced as the material peeled off. Only at her bra and pants did modesty make her try and resist, but Seton simply pushed her hands aside. He slipped off the flimsy underclothes, and studied her naked body with concerned eyes.

'You've got some nasty bruises and cuts,' he said. 'But those had better wait until tomorrow.' He laid his hand against her stomach. 'And your skin's clammy. Better dry off a little before you get into bed. Go and warm yourself by the brazier for a minute or two.' Madge obeyed, exhaustion overcoming her shyness, and stood in front of the flickering flames, holding her palms out to the delicious warmth, a slender, fairylike figure in the orange light. The heat was like balm on her cold skin, helping to ease away the ache of bruises and abrasions. Somehow, it seemed natural to be naked with him.

'When I saw the Land Rover,' he said quietly, pulling his own clothes off, 'I was certain you were dead, Madge. It's a miracle you weren't smashed to pieces in there.' She turned her head to smile at him.

'The Mimyin decided to have mercy,' she quipped.

'Somebody decided to have mercy,' he said, his face grave. 'I'd never have forgiven myself if you'd been really hurt, Madge. I should never have left you, not just for the sake of some damned film.'

She smiled to herself at the uncharacteristic words, then remembered the crash. 'All our gear must have been destroyed in the car?' she asked. He nodded.

'Completely. And I had to leave both the cameras at the wreck.'

'Oh no!' she sighed, remembering. 'The film . . . I've really messed everything up, haven't I?'

'You were extremely brave,' he said gently. 'As for the film I shot, I took it out of the camera and brought it with us.' She watched the ripple of muscle on his torso as he thrust one hand into the pocket of his jeans. 'Here it is.' She stared at the flat aluminium can in his hand.

'Will it be okay?'

'I don't know,' he confessed, dropping it on the sideboard and pulling off the rest of his wet clothes. 'And right now, I don't care.'

'Can this really be Seton Chambers talking?' Madge smiled sleepily. The brazier spluttered softly in the deep silence. The Lamas had strewn some aromatic herb in the fire, and its strange smell perfumed the air with a hint of pine.

Then he, too, was naked. She turned to him, her face soft, her senses swaying at the sight of him. With a mysterious smile, Seton held out his arms to her, and she gasped softly, deep in her throat, as their naked bodies came together. She was slim in his arms, the tender peaks of her breasts pressing against the hard muscle of his chest, her hips shamelessly pressed to his, drinking in his warmth and power. She caressed his back with slow hands, adoring him as she had never adored anything or anyone in her life, intoxicated by the strength of his embrace.

'We made it,' he said huskily, his fingers combing her damp hair. 'We made it . . .'

She raised her lips to his, her heavy lids fluttering closed as his lips probed the sweetness of her inner mouth. Then, as the first flame of passion thrust between them, he pushed her away with the same secret smile.

'Not now.' He led her to the vast bed, and threw back the heavy Tibetan-style quilt. 'In,' he commanded.

The soft raw cotton sheets were ecstasy against her tired limbs. He slid down beside her, and she reached out for him as naturally as though she had done it all her life. He pulled her close, pillowing her head on his chest. A languorous warmth ironed her face smooth, thickening the words on her tongue even as she tried to utter them. She drank in the warm velvet of his skin, his man-smell infinitely comforting in her nostrils.

Sleep came without pain or dreams.

It was ten o'clock the next morning by the time Madge dragged herself into wakefulness to face the steaming bowl of *tsampa* that a smiling Lama had just put at her bedside. She listened as the monk walked quietly out and closed the door, then lay in a semi-daze for a while, her mind slipping in and out of dreams. In the morning sun, the orange-painted room was luminous and warm. She stirred slowly, realising that Seton wasn't there any more. She must have spent the whole night in his arms. And oh—every bone in her body seemed to ache, and her muscles were as stiff as boards. Otherwise, though, she seemed to have no lasting ill-effects from the accident. She struggled painfully upright, looking for Seton.

He was sitting on a small couch at the foot of the bed, one golden shoulder emerging from the wine-coloured gown he wore. A similar gown, several sizes too large for her, had been laid on the sideboard. Seton raised his bowl of *tsampa* in a semi-ironic salute.

'So you *are* alive.' His smile spread that sweet warmth through her, and she smiled back, her ache for him momentarily overcoming her physical aches.

'Just about, anyway.' She met the amused blue eyes,

then dropped her gaze as she remembered her own nakedness, and pulled the quilt up to her chin. 'Last night I dreamed we were in Kanchen monastery. Isn't that odd?'

He smiled at her feeble little joke. 'Extremely odd. How do you feel this morning?'

'Battered,' she admitted. 'And you?'

'Not bad.' Which was an understatement, she reflected with a touch of envy. His golden skin glowed with health, and the darkening of beard on his jaw only made him all the more devastatingly attractive in the morning light. She dropped her eyes from his wickedly handsome grin, and examined her bowl of *tsampa*. 'I'm starving. But—ugh!'

'You get quite a taste for this stuff,' he said calmly, spooning up the last of his bowl.

'I think I'll skip it,' she decided.

One eyebrow arched warningly.

'Eat. You won't get anything else in a Tibetan monastery, Copleigh. This is their staple diet.'

'I know—I found that out last night. Yak-butter tea and salted barley.' She pulled another face, but started eating nevertheless. 'Last night,' she said between spoonfuls, 'I seem to remember you calling me Madge. Have I been demoted to "Copleigh" again?'

'Anyone as dissipated-looking as you should think herself lucky to be called anything,' he replied coolly. He set the bowl down and stood up, giving her a glimpse of his broad chest as he rearranged the Tibetan gown around his body. 'You look as though you've been pulled through a hedge backwards.'

'You found me attractive enough to kiss last night,' she said shortly, rebellious green eyes flicking up to meet his.

'I'm used to you—the Lamas aren't. So—when you've finished your breakfast, girl, we'll get you cleaned up.'

'"We"?' Madge queried warily.

'While you were sleeping peacefully,' he informed her, 'I've been busy learning sign language. Our hosts are bringing you a little surprise—I hope. I want to see how badly you've been hurt. And our friend the Abbot has kindly lent us these.' She followed his pointing finger to the tray on the gilt sideboard. There were a pile of bandages on it, and a small bottle.

'What's in there?' she asked.

'Tibetan medicine. Our friends didn't explain exactly what. Herbal remedies, most likely, going back centuries. They'll probably do as much good as any Western antibiotics.'

'Oh.' Her dubious expression went unnoticed. There was a gentle tap at the door, and Seton opened it. Three Lamas dragged in something large and obviously heavy, which gave off clouds of steam.

'A bath?' she blinked.

'*The* bath, I should think.' There was a rapid exchange in Tibetan, which meant little to either of them, though the import was clearly friendly. More understandably, the Lamas also laid out heavy towels and a bar of coarse-looking soap. Pressing his hands together, Seton bowed thanks to the old men, and they smiled their way out.

It was an ancient galvanised iron hip-bath, its proportions suggesting it had been designed for a bather of truly elephantine proportions. 'They must have been up since dawn boiling all this water,' Seton commented. He took the breakfast bowl from her hands and smiled. 'Come.'

'I'll bath myself,' Madge suggested hastily.

'Not in your present state.' An ironic expression settled over the authoritative mouth. 'And if you're worried about corrupting me, I'm inured to the temptations of your voluptuousness, Copleigh. Come on!'

Unhappily, she sat up and her whole body protested sharply at the movement. She looked up at Seton, her emerald eyes contrasting against her still-pale skin and red lips, then rose to her feet, letting the quilt slip unwillingly away from her slender body. Stiffness and bruises made her gasp silently. Dear heaven, she felt like an old woman!

'Now you see what I mean,' he said calmly. But his hands were gentle as he guided her to the tub.

Her embarrassment about being naked in front of him receded slightly. She put one foot into the water, and winced.

'It's too hot!'

'That'll help the bruises. Be brave.' Slowly gasping as strained muscles came into play, Madge lowered herself into the blissfully hot water until she was sitting breast-deep. Her face dewed with steam, she leaned back against the tub, and let out her breath in a long sigh. It was true; the hot water was easing away the pains, loosening up her whole body as though there'd been ice in her veins.

She opened dreamy eyes. Seton was leaning on the edge of the tub, watching her with a strange expression on his face. She covered the tense, dark nipples of her breasts with her arms. 'I'm not sure it's very seemly to be so exposed before a gentleman,' she said with a wobbly smile.

'I'm no gentleman.' His mouth softened. 'Feeling better now?'

'Much.'

'Good. Now—just relax.' The heat had melted her will completely, and she merely nodded. He scooped water up with a huge enamelled jug, commanded her to close her eyes, and poured the water in a glittering cascade over her hair. She smelt something sweet, and then he was lathering her hair, the feeling of his sure fingers good against her scalp. She submitted in a kind of trance, revelling in the luxurious sensations of having her hair washed and thoroughly rinsed.

She leaned forward, half asleep, her hair dripping over her eyes as he soaped her back, then rinsed the fine skin with clean water.

'I remind myself of a cat,' she said dreamily. 'Every time you touch me, I want to purr.'

'Indeed.' She wondered whether he was smiling. 'In that case, I'd better leave you to wash the rest on your own.'

'I didn't mean that.' She pushed the wet hair out of her face, and looked at him. 'Or are you afraid of what might happen if you arouse my slumbering passions?'

'I see a night's rest has restored you to your usual form,' he growled. 'Here's the soap, Copleigh.'

Yet despite his gruffness, Madge sensed something in Seton, a tension that told her for some reason she had at last got through that iron barrier around his feelings. Could it be that her nakedness was disturbing his equilibrium ever so slightly? Just how tough *was* that famous self-control? A surge of inner mischief made her shake her head.

'I'm much too stiff to wash myself,' she said piteously. 'Please do it for me.'

The deep blue eyes raked hers for any sign of laughter, but she composed her face into an expression of feeble suffering. She was safe, after all—there wasn't much that could happen between them in their present battered conditions, in a Tibetan hip-bath, with tonsured monks flitting in and out! It was delicious to feel that, just for once, it was he, and not she, who was discomfited! He shrugged, still looking slightly uncomfortable, and pushed the wine-coloured sleeves away from his arms.

'Okay. Sit up, if you can.' She obeyed, dropping her gaze modestly to cover her inward amusement—and the fact that her heart had begun to thump. In silence, he

soaped her sides and flanks, the smell of sandalwood
sweet around them. As soon as he touched her skin,
though, she knew what a bad mistake she had made.
She had simply wanted to tease him, maybe (if she was
being honest) to remind him of how powerful the
magnetism between them was. But the touch of his
hands on her breasts was an emotional shock she was
totally unprepared for, and her teeth sank into her
lower lip as his strong, firm fingers spread soap across
her wet skin.

She had never in her life really learned to think of her
body as an erotic thing, something beautiful that could
give and receive pleasure; but now, the sheer sexiness of
what he was doing shook Madge's being down to her
soul. Seton's hands were big enough to cup her neat
breasts completely, and she knew he would be as
acutely aware as she herself of the hardening peaks
against his palms. The almost violent yearning that
erupted inside her made her too shy to look up at him
and see whether any of her own feelings would be
reflected in his face——

Until the movements of his hands stopped any
pretence of indifference, and became a voluptuous, slow
caress that brought his thumbs sliding hard across the
dark, eager stars of her nipples. She arched her neck
with a deep shudder, and stared straight into the naked
desire of his eyes. Her hands crept over his, cupping his
palms closer over her aching breasts. If only she could
make him believe in the passion that held them both in
its wonderful spell, convince him that this physical
desire was really a manifestation of the emotional love
that went much, much deeper . . .

'You don't know what you're doing to me,' she
whispered shakily.

'I know what I'm doing to myself,' he said, his deep
voice rough. 'I should know better by now.' He slid his
hands round her shoulders, and drew her forward so

that he could kiss her moist lips with almost harsh passion. Then he drew a breath that sounded shaky to Madge's burning ears. 'You'd better wash yourself from here on,' he ordered, releasing her and standing up. 'I'll have a look at your wounds when you're done.'

Feeling as though a powerful electric current had passed through all her muscles, Madge sank weakly back in the water. So much for her little games! Yet she had seen the desire in his eyes, the naked passion she had aroused in him, and that stayed with her like a warm glow inside.

Seton stood silently at the window as she washed herself, the red gown pulled close around him. Her pulse-rate subsided slowly as she rinsed off the soap, and she was feeling distinctly uncertain when at last she asked timidly, 'Could you pass me a towel, please?'

He didn't smile as he draped the rough-feeling towel round her shoulders. Her legs felt slightly stronger as she stepped out of the bath, huddling into the towel. The hot water had done her good, after all. But there was a tension between them that could be felt in the air, a sense of being coiled like a spring, waiting for the moment of release.

She sat tautly on the bed as he examined the various cuts and abrasions on her back.

'There's a nasty bruise on your back,' he told her, his fingers exploring her skin gently. 'And you've got some deep cuts. I'm going to dress this one on your shoulder.'

She nodded, and pulled a slight face as the medicine he dabbed on stung the tender skin.

'Sore?'

'Only a bit.' He pressed a bandage into place. 'I didn't mean to make you angry just now,' she said in a low voice. 'You're right—we should know better by now.'

'It isn't your fault.' He picked up her hands, and examined the cuts on her fingers. Then he looked up into her eyes, smiling a little crookedly. 'I want you, Madge—you know that.'

'Yes,' she said shakily. 'Trouble is, I don't know how to handle that, Seton. I've never been wanted by—by someone like you before. I feel so frightened of you half the time——' She tucked the towel over the tops of her breasts, her face reddening. 'I just feel that ever since we met, I've been doing one wrong thing after another. I've been a fool, and on top of that, I've allowed this—this tension to grow up between us.'

'That's not your doing either,' he said quietly. 'I've felt that tension with you for weeks, Madge. Maybe even ever since you came to work at Studio Seven.'

'Truly?' she asked, dark lashes widening round jade-green eyes.

'It happens sometimes,' he said, touching her cheek with his fingertips. 'It means there's a strong physical attraction between us, something we can't do anything about.'

'Is that all it means?' she asked quietly.

His mouth became wry.

'That's all, Madge.'

'It isn't—anything special?'

'You're special,' he said huskily. The words seemed to grate out, as though he found difficulty in saying them. 'Your eyes are special, and your lips are special, and your skin's like satin. And you do something very special to me, every time I look at you. But emotionally—no, it isn't special.' His eyes were locked on hers, a contact that was deep, almost primaeval in the way it affected her. 'It's not special at all.' With an effort, he turned away, and picked up the medicine-bottle again. 'Now, let's attend to your cuts. Where else are you hurt?'

Unhappily, Madge unwound the towel from round her shoulders and showed him the long graze on her ribs. Seeming to ignore her naked breasts, he dabbed the aromatic-smelling medicine on her skin.

'That won't need a bandage.' His voice was still rough, his brows drawn dark over his eyes. 'Anywhere else?'

She nodded, and silently lifted the towel to reveal her left hip, where something sharp had torn through her jeans and pierced the flesh beneath during her hectic tumble down the mountainside. He cleaned the cut carefully with the medicine, then taped a bandage over it.

'You risked your life to find me,' he said quietly. 'If the petrol in the tanks had ignited——' He cut the sentence off sharply, and glanced at the deep cut on the inside of her thigh, just visible although her knees were tightly pressed together.

'Let me look.' She bit her lip, hesitating. 'Come on,' he snapped, 'this is no time for stupid modesty!'

With scarlet cheeks, Madge tucked the towel between her legs, and parted her thighs slightly. Impatiently, Seton knelt down to examine the cut. The harsh lines of his face softened as he saw how painfully she had been cut.

'Poor kid,' he muttered. She gritted her teeth as he brushed the wound gently with the stinging medicine. 'At least it's clean,' he commented. 'Thank God this didn't touch the artery, or you'd have bled to death in the Land Rover. I'm not going to cover this, Madge— it'll heal better that way.' He tended the cut with firm, compassionate fingers—then, unexpectedly, he leaned down and kissed the satiny skin next to the wound. His lips were warm, tender. She couldn't stop the shudder inside her, half of pain, half of ecstasy, and her eyes were closed as he draped the towel back over her thighs, and came beside her to take her in his arms.

'I can't believe it's nothing more than sex,' she said in a low urgent voice. 'I can't believe it, and I don't believe you believe it either!'

'I told you before,' he said harshly, 'the only relationships I have with women end at the bedroom door. Why can't you be warned? There's no room for sentiment in my life, child. There never will be.'

'Why not?' She opened eyes that were dark with pain to stare into his. 'Why not? Because of Lana? You told me yourself you didn't love her. You've been in mourning for five years over what happened to her, Seton—and there's not enough time in the world for mourning. Not if you want to live as well!'

His arms tightened around her, as though to crush what she was saying, negate it; but she clung to him, her voice throbbing with the love bursting inside her heart.

'You're afraid that you can't love again—but you *can*. It's time to start again, start to love, start to live——'

'You're asking me for something I can't give you,' he said painfully. He took her face in his hands, the muscles across his shoulders rigid with strain. 'Darling Madge, if only the world were as simple as you say it is! But you're building a castle in the air around yourself, and when it falls, you're going to be so hurt ...' He brushed her obstinate mouth with his thumb. 'It's an illusion, Madge.'

'My love for you is real,' she said, her eyes blurring. If only she had had the gift of eloquence, the ability to show him just how much love was in her heart? 'That's all I know. I want you, I've always wanted you—but as my man, not just my lover. I want to spend the rest of my life beside you, give you the children you deserve——'

'*Stop!*' There was such agony in his eyes that she bowed her head against his, her arms tight round his neck. 'Don't say these things to me, Madge. They mean too much.'

Knowing that she was closer to him than she'd ever

been made Madge desperate. 'Then accept them! Accept me!'

'For how long?' His voice was bitter. 'A week? A month? I care too much for you to want to wound you. If you only knew how much I wanted to believe that this was real, and not an illusion—if you only knew how much it's costing me to keep you at a distance, how much it's cost me already——' He shook his head. 'For God's sake, Madge—protect yourself from me. Don't want to walk into the fire.'

She looked at him helplessly, knowing this was something she'd never get over. 'I've been walking through fire for you for half my life,' she said wryly. He might as well have forbidden the sea to embrace the shore; deep in her heart, Madge felt the inevitability of her feelings for him. Loving him wasn't, as he seemed to think, a matter of choice. It wasn't anything she could control—it controlled her, making her unique.

There was a knock at the door, and their eyes met, tormented, adoring.

'No more, sweetheart,' he said gently.

'Then just promise me this,' she said in a quick whisper. 'Promise you won't say no for ever. Not now. Promise we can talk about it again when we get back to London.'

'There's no point,' he said roughly.

'*Promise!*' She clenched her fingers in his thick dark hair, her eyes almost wild with urgency. '*Promise!*'

He opened his mouth to retort—and suddenly that bone-melting, battered grin crossed his face.

'All right, Copleigh, I'll promise that.' He raised a warning finger at her glowing face as he rose to open the door. 'No more than that. We'll talk—and you'll build up no false hopes or expectations.'

She nodded, brimming with happiness. Seton opened the door. Standing there was a youngish monk, and behind him the Abbot, resplendent in his red robes.

They bowed all round, and then the young monk held out a book to Seton. The cover read *Tibetan–English Phrase-Book*.

He took it with another bow, and flipped it open.

'Ah,' he said. 'Now we're in business.'

CHAPTER NINE

THE gathering storm was an awesome sight. The cloud-mass, luminous with sunlight, spread its wings in immense grandeur over the peaks of the Himalayas. Soon the sun itself was obliterated in this apocalyptic meeting between the sky and the mountains. The clouds descended like the vast army of some Tibetan deity, their shape ever-changing as the winds and the fitful sunlight played over them. The elemental savagery of the scene was deeply thrilling, and the watchers in the small projection-room sat in stunned silence, transfixed by the shifting play of light, the implacable rolling advance of the thunderheads.

Daphne Hunt, one of Studio Seven's most experienced programme editors, and an old hand at Seton Chambers' films, turned in her chair, eyes screwed up against the smoke from the inevitable cigarette in her mouth.

'I take it this was shot just before Madge's accident?' she hissed.

Beside Madge, Seton unhooked his feet from the seat in front, and sat upright. 'Yes. Madge was asleep in the car, further down the pass.'

'It's fantastic stuff,' Daphne marvelled, turning back to the screen. She and her assistant editor, Bruce Mackintosh, scribbled busily in their notepads, planning the way the programme was to take shape in the cutting-room.

'You were crazy not to come down immediately when you saw it coming towards you,' Madge said to Seton in a furious whisper. 'God! If I'd known you were sitting up there, calmly filming the coming storm, I might not have bothered coming to look for you!'

'Crazy,' he nodded. She caught the glint of his smile in the semi-darkness of the projection room. 'But as soon as I got to the top of the pass, and saw the storm gathering, I knew that this was going to be perfect for the film.'

'So you couldn't resist it.' She shook her head, turning back to the magnificent photography unfolding on the screen. 'Sometimes I think that if you fell out of an aeroplane, Seton, you'd film the view on the way down rather than open your parachute!'

'It's called professionalism,' he told her drily. 'You might pick it up one day, who knows?'

A burst of applause as the lights went up cut short Madge's retort. The ten or twelve people privileged enough to be at this first showing of the unedited 'raw' film of the Tibetan trip were clearly very excited by what they'd seen. There was a clamour of questions about Tibet, the Lamas, the Potala, which Seton fielded in his usual unruffled way. Madge watched him with a strange mixture of pride and irony in her heart.

This was what it must be like to be Seton Chambers—even the first showings of your raw film became a television event; everything that you touched turned to gold. She compared the modest obscurity in which she and Charlie Molesworth usually laboured to this excited, impromptu party. And the film hadn't even been edited yet.

Someone thumped her on the shoulder, oblivious to her wince of pain as a still-unhealed bruise protested sharply.

'Congratulations, Madge! This film is going to be fantastic. Wonderful stuff, wonderful!' She smiled appreciation, and murmured some disclaimer. Daphne Hunt, clipboard in hand, settled next to her, her lived-in face decorated with its usual cigarette.

'Well done, Madge. It's going to be a winner.'

'Oh, it was all Seton's doing,' she shrugged in return. 'But thanks, anyway.'

'That's not true,' said Daphne, raising her eyebrows in surprise. 'Your shots in the temples are simply beautiful, child. Sheer poetry, from start to finish.' She dragged deep on her cigarette, plucked it out of her mouth, and exhaled a great plume. Her eyes were shrewd behind the gold-rimmed spectacles. 'Altogether, the film's unique. Not just because of the romantic subject matter, either. Because you and Seton make a brilliant team.'

Someone interrupted with eager congratulations, and Madge smiled brightly at him, not really taking in the praise, then turned back to Daphne.

'You mean that?'

'Mean it?' The cigarette went back for another deep drag. 'Don't be silly—you've just seen the raw film for yourself. Even though it hasn't been edited—and believe me, it's going to be a non-stop pleasure editing this film—the expertise, the teamwork is obvious. This is one of the most successful combinations ever to come out of Studio Seven. I've a shrewd feeling that Seton's going to ask you to work with him on the Arctic cruise film.'

'The one being planned now?' Madge shook her head sharply. 'You're mistaken, Daphne. Seton doesn't need anyone working with him.'

'He's been looking for a working partner for a couple of years now,' said Daphne, watching Madge's face. 'Didn't you know?'

'No, I didn't,' Madge blinked.

'Well, you don't look very excited about it,' Daphne smiled. 'Seton Chambers is the greatest film-maker around, Madge. There's no one to equal his work in the field—there never has been. If he does want you to work with him again, you'll be heading straight for the top yourself. Not bad for—what is it, twenty-four?'

'But Seton's not going to ask me to work with him again,' said Madge, shaking her head. 'This was a one-off thing, a fluke. It won't ever happen again.'

Someone butted in to congratulate her on the film before Daphne could reply, and while she was busy fielding questions, Bruce Mackintosh prised Daphne away from the conversation. Madge glanced over the shoulders to where Seton was nodding at something one of the senior producers was saying.

Seton's partner? It wasn't possible. Seton was a lone wolf, a man who hunted alone. He'd never needed anyone, never would. And she couldn't just desert Charlie, even if by some miracle Seton *did* want her to join him. She and Charlie had been the original team, not she and Seton . . .

Besides—with Seton's attitudes towards working relationships, becoming his partner would be effectively kissing goodbye to any chance of becoming anything more to him. The thought made her smile with a touch of irony. What chance did she have, anyway?

'You're very kind,' she murmured to her admirer, and began to gather her handbag and notes, preparatory to going up to her office. There was work to do. Her back still ached slightly, five days after their return from Tibet, but the mysterious medicines had worked wonders on her. The monks at Kanchen had been wonderfully kind, guiding the two of them back down to the village the next day, and even arranging to have the Land Rover towed back to Xigaze for the extensive repairs it needed.

She had wept uncontrollably as they left Lhasa forty-eight hours later—not, as they had planned, by car, but on a hastily-booked airline flight to the People's Republic, and thence to Bombay and Heathrow. So much had happened to her in Tibet, both good and bad, so much experience that had changed her inside for ever.

Nor could she ever forget that it was in Tibet she had first found love. The only love she was ever going to have.

Yet the extraordinary voyage had ended on such an uncertain note, with nothing resolved, nothing settled. She looked across the room to the only man she had ever loved, aching to speak to him, touch him. A press of people blocked her from his sight.

Yearning for Seton, she turned her back resolutely on the slowly-emptying room, and took the lift up to her office. There had scarcely been a moment of privacy between them since their arrival, not only because they had both been hectically busy, but also because Madge herself had returned to find herself in the midst of a family crisis.

Tyrone Copleigh was back in England, physically and emotionally worn out. Her mother had taken Madge to see her father the first night she'd arrived in London. She had been shocked at the worn, pathetic figure in the expensive nursing-home bed. Her mother had filled Madge in privately on the details, her tone a mixture of bitterness and compassion. Her father's love-affair with the German starlet had ended disastrously. She had taken him, as Olivia Copleigh put it, 'for the ride of the century', using up his money and his emotions with equal callousness. On the edge of a nervous collapse, the ageing film-star had been struck down with pneumonia—and had been left alone, literally penniless, and seriously ill in his Californian villa.

Olivia, with an unwonted gesture of affection for the man she had once loved, had paid for her ex-husband to be flown out to Britain and hospitalised at Kennilwood. Tyrone Copleigh, his handsome face now thin and drawn, and much of his self-assurance gone, had responded with a touching gratitude.

Madge grimaced as she sat down behind her desk,

and stared blankly around the dusty, deserted-looking office. What a weird feeling it had been—the three of them, together again after all these years. She had been tempted by emotionalism to give way to tears in the bright, white private ward, but had resisted. She couldn't afford any more tears for her parents, couldn't afford to place any more hope in their wayward natures. Yet the strange feeling that the family was knitting itself together again had persisted in her mind for the past few days.

She was going to see them again tonight, another fraught, tense hospital visit. So much to think about, so much to do . . .

The urgent clamour of the telephone interrupted her thoughts, and she picked it up to hear Charlie Molesworth's familiar voice on the line.

'Charlie!' She sat up in delight. 'How are you?'

'Recovering,' he laughed. 'I'll be up and about soon, according to the quack. Hey, I hear your film's going to be a raving success, the biggest thing since *The Whale's Song*. I knew you'd do it.'

'It hasn't even got to the cutting-room yet,' she protested—then, with a pang of guilt, 'Look, Charlie, I'm so sorry I haven't been to see you yet. It's been one thing after another since I got back, and my parents have been keeping me busy——'

'You don't have to apologise,' he interrupted happily. 'I know exactly what it's like. Listen, is it true you had some kind of accident in Tibet?'

'Nothing serious,' she lied. 'Just a few bruises.'

'That's all right, then. Some fool told me you rolled a Land Rover down Everest, or something. So—what was it like working with The Chief? An education?'

'You could say that,' she replied ironically. 'He's full of surprises. I know I've learned a great deal, anyway.'

'I'll bet,' he chuckled. 'I take it you don't still hate his guts?'

'I never did,' Madge sighed. 'You sound in remarkably high spirits, by the way. Won the pools?'

'Oh—er, no.' Some of Charlie's elation dimmed. 'I—well, I've had some good news, that's all.' He cleared his throat. 'Or it would be good news if I could take it up.'

'That sounds intriguing,' Madge smiled.

'Yeah. You know Alaric Joyce, the American producer?'

'Of course.'

'He's invited me to go to Los Angeles for three years to work with him on a wildlife series for N.B.C. All expenses paid for me and Doreen—free house, car, the lot.'

'But Charlie!' Flabbergasted, she could only shake her head. 'That's *wonderful!* Oh, I'm so pleased for you!'

'I'm going to turn it down, of course,' he said. 'But it's nice to be asked. He said he's always liked my work and——'

'Turn it down?' she yelled. 'What on earth for?'

'Why, because of us, Madge. You and me. We're partners, remember? What we've got is worth any Los Angeles sinecure.'

Madge's full mouth set into its most stubborn line. 'Charlie, listen to me. What we've got—what we *had*—is an exciting, experimental partnership. We've made some good films. But let's face it, we're still on the fringes of the business, and we will be for years, no matter how many prizes we win. We've never made more than a pittance out of our work.'

'But——'

'With Alaric Joyce you'll be right at the heart of the American television scene.' Her green eyes glinted. 'And if you think I'm going to hold you back from what's rightfully yours, Charlie, you better think again! You deserve this, if anyone does. I'm *so* pleased for you—

and if you don't get to the top in five years, I shall be very surprised!'

'I couldn't just walk out on you, Madge.' The strain in his voice was audible, and Madge smiled.

'Tell me, Charlie—what does Doreen think about all this?'

'Doreen?' He cleared his throat uncomfortably. 'She's pleased, naturally, but——'

'Pleased? Three years in Los Angeles, a free mansion and a great big American car? *And* her husband working for the East Coast's top producer? I'll bet she's pleased!'

'Yeah, but she feels exactly the way I do——'

'She does not,' Madge retorted firmly. 'She's got more brains than that. I'll bet a hundred pounds that she told you I'd understand, and that I'd be only too delighted to see you making a success of your career— without me. Am I wrong?'

'Oh, Madge,' he sighed.

'Well, she's dead right. That's exactly how I feel, partner. This is your big break, and you have to seize it right now.'

The door of her office opened, and her heart jolted as Seton walked in, immaculate in his dark suit. He perched himself on the desk opposite, watching her with a hint of amusement in those sapphire-bright eyes. She sat up hastily. 'You have to accept, Charlie. It's so important to you and Doreen. Who knows, you might even decide to start your family there, in all that lovely sun!'

'Madge, you're the sweetest person I've ever known,' he said, and she could hear the emotion in his voice. 'I feel such a heel about this.'

'Don't.' Her eyes met Seton's, and she looked away quickly. 'Have I persuaded you?'

'I don't know whether I'll really be better off without you, Madgie,' he said wryly. 'But if you think I should go, then I will.'

'Wonderful—I'm so excited for you! I can't wait to talk it over with you and Doreen, and hear all your plans. Can I come round tomorrow?'

'Any time,' he said, still sounding choky.

'Around six, then. Look, Charlie, I have to go. Give my love to Doreen. See you.' She hung up, and tried a small smile on Seton. 'Sorry to keep you waiting.'

'Not at all,' he said gravely. 'I guessed you'd be here when you disappeared from the projection room.' He nodded at the phone. 'Good news?'

'Very,' she said, feeling weirdly shy and awkward with him. 'My partner's been offered a fantastic new job in the States.'

'And that's good news?' His expression of elegant surprise rang alarm bells somewhere in Madge's mind. 'Doesn't that mean you'll be left on your own?'

'Yes,' she shrugged, watching him cautiously. 'But it's a great chance for Charlie—and I do have resources of my own.'

'Such as?'

'I could work solo,' she said, staring defiantly into Seton's face. 'The way you do.'

'That's a thought,' he purred. The Cheshire-cat smile wrapped sensual arms around her, and her pulse-rate jumped. 'They're all predicting great things for you back in the projection-room, Copleigh. You'll go far, so they say.'

'That's nice to know,' she said, keeping her expression neutral. 'I hope I live up to expectations.'

'You will.' He turned, and walked to the window. The summer sun through the blind cast bars of gold across his face as he looked out. 'Going solo is one way of doing it. But it's not easy.'

'You seem to have managed,' she smiled. How odd it was, talking to him in this rather stilted, civilised way—when they'd shared a naked bath beside a brazier halfway up Kanchenjunga together!

'So far,' he said obliquely. 'Working on your own is lonely. It means self-sacrifice, dedication, abstinence. It means giving up all the things that other people hold precious. Like happiness. Love.' He turned to her, hands in his pockets. 'I've done it for years, I know what I'm talking about. To work alone, you have to live alone, think alone—be alone in the very core of your being. Sometimes that strengthens people. Sometimes it withers them up inside, so that they forget how to feel. Forget how to feel, and you forget how to live.'

Fascinated, Madge watched his tall, powerful figure. She hadn't heard him talk so intimately and frankly about himself since that night in Lhasa. Why was he saying all this to her?

'Are you saying I shouldn't strike out alone?' she asked quietly, aching to know what was in his mind. Perhaps, in a roundabout way, he was preparing to tell her it was all over between them. The thought chilled her to the soul. Maybe this was the talk he'd promised they would have once they got back.

'I'm just saying that there are more important things in this life than work.' Seton walked slowly across the office, his eyes introspective. 'To be alone is to risk forgetting how the other humans live and feel—and in the end, that'll kill your work as well as everything else. It'll become sterile, and die.'

'But your work is full of feeling,' she protested. 'Every frame is bursting with passion, Seton. There's nothing sterile about you. There's only strength. And self-control. I admire that about you and your work. No, more—I love it.' She met his glance obstinately. 'It gives everything else meaning.'

'Yet we all have to learn from one another,' he said gently. 'I teach you. You teach me. That can't go on in isolation.'

Hope surged in her like a wave. Was he saying he needed her, that there might be a chance for their love?

She prayed it was so, but bit the fear and the hope back firmly. 'I never thought I'd hear you arguing like this,' she smiled. 'You—always such a loner, so disciplined. In Lhasa you told me it had to be that way. Have I really taught you otherwise?'

'I need a partner,' he said, not answering her question. 'A co-producer, someone I can work with on a full-time basis—as equals. Someone to exchange ideas with, to share the work with. And I'm asking you to be that person.'

Madge sat back in her chair, her mind spinning. So— it was true, as Daphne had said. But it wasn't what she had longed for. The pain showed in her darkening eyes. He needed a partner. Not love, not the life she could give him. Just her talent. The irony was raw in her mouth. Oh, how she would have been thrilled by this invitation a year or two ago! But now——

'You once told me that you deliberately cut me dead because you didn't want my talent to get swamped by your influence,' she said, her voice sounding unhappy and strained to her own ears. He nodded, watching her eyes. 'Doesn't that still hold true?'

'No. You've grown up. I've watched you for a long time, though you didn't know it. Ever since you came up to me in the corridor, a wide-eyed kid of twenty, and naïvely told me you thought *The Whale's Song* was a wonderful film. I didn't watch you out of vanity, just because you liked my work. I watched you because you gave me a feeling, a kind of inner conviction that you were real.'

'Real?' she queried, her eyes soft.

'A real person among all the fakes and the phoneys. Someone with feelings, prepared to commit herself, no matter whether she got hurt in the process or not. A rare quality—a quality I noticed time and time again while we were in Tibet. And sitting down there this morning, eighteen months later, and watching the film you'd shot in Tibet, I knew you'd come into your own at last.' He smiled at her, leaning back against the desk. 'Not another Seton Chambers imitator. Not another clever brat with a few flashy, shallow ideas. A truly gifted film-maker, with an exceptional talent—and a deep maturity of vision.'

The blood rushed into her cheeks, and she turned away abruptly to hide the fact that her eyes were glistening with tears. It was as though she had been waiting for the past half-decade for that recognition, those simple words of praise from the one person she cared more about than anyone else in the world. What a morning it had been for mixed emotions; if only he knew how he was tearing her up inside . . .

'I don't expect you to come up with an instant answer,' he went on, his voice quiet. 'Not even over the next few months. But I want you to come with me to the Arctic circle in August, and work with me on a new documentary. We'll be operating from an old-time schooner—just you and me, and a team of two sound-recordists. And Lilian Topping, the naturalist. And by the time we get back I want you to have made your mind up, one way or the other.'

Madge nodded, too full to speak much. Sweet heaven, if only he wanted her to be more than his partner, his workmate . . .

'If the Arctic film works out,' he went on, watching her profile, 'I think I'd like to leave Studio Seven.'

She smiled ironically at his ability to keep surprising her. 'Leave?'

'I like beginnings. When I started Studio Seven four years ago, with a few friends from here and there, I wanted to create something new in the television industry, something really different. You know something about why I make films, about the way I see the world by now. I wanted to make that dream come true.'

'You succeeded.' She turned to him, loving him so

much it made her ache. 'You've done so much with this company!'

'Sure. And now it's growing into another vast television corporation. We're buying new centres in Europe, employing new staff, making thousands. Our budget this year is almost six million.' He shrugged. 'I like being disgustingly rich. I'm not going to turn into a monk overnight. But I also need to be free—and Studio Seven's stopped letting me be free.'

'Why?'

'I have no time for films any more.' Restlessly he turned away. 'I've become a sort of supercharged director, shuttling around the world with a briefcase full of incomprehensible documents, talking to boring fat men in thousand-dollar suits.' His sensual mouth curled in disgust. 'When you taunted me about wanting to get back into the field, all those weeks ago, you were dead right. I want to make films, the way I've always done. The difference is that now I want to make them with you. In a relatively small, vigorous company. On our own.'

Her emotions twisted and tore inside her. Did he really think she would be able to work by his side, year after year, her soul yearning for him? Did he want her to become a sterile old maid for him? She wasn't sure whether she could face that . . .

'I'll think about it,' she promised tautly, not trusting herself even to look at him. He nodded.

'From what I heard when I came in, I take it you're not too upset about Charlie Molesworth going to work for Alaric Joyce?'

'No, I'm delighted,' she replied, then froze as his words sank in. She turned staring green eyes on him. 'You? *You* arranged this invitation?'

'Alaric Joyce is a good friend. And when he asked me whether I knew a good young cameraman, I had no hesitation in recommending Charlie.' He watched her carefully. 'Are you angry with me?'

Suddenly everything boiled up inside Madge, an uncontrollable rush of passionate anger—anger at his indifference to her feelings, anger at the way he managed to shake her to her core, anger at her own irreversible love for him. 'Angry?' She rose, disbelief turning to fury in her pale face. 'You're damn right I'm angry!'

His face tightened. 'May I ask why?'

'Because, Seton Chambers, you damn well take the biscuit!' She was shaking with the force of her feelings, her voice almost out of control. 'What in God's name makes you think you've got the right to manipulate other people's lives? What makes you think you can just shuffle people round the world to suit your own plans?'

'Alaric Joyce is Charlie's big chance,' he said calmly. 'Just as this is yours.'

'You flatter yourself,' she snarled, shaking with emotion. 'I'm not going anywhere with you! I wouldn't go to the end of the street with someone who behaves like you do. You've just broken up an eighteen-month partnership without blinking! God, I was right first time—you're as cold as a machine! You don't give a damn about anyone's feelings, do you? All that talk just now about needing other people—that was just to soft-soap me, wasn't it? So you could mould me into whatever plans you had for me!'

'There's a certain hypocrisy in what you say,' he retorted sharply. 'I thought you were so delighted that Charlie Molesworth was getting a real break?'

'Not when it's all been engineered behind his back!'

'There was no engineering involved,' he snapped. 'Alaric asked for my recommendation, I gave it. That's all.'

'That isn't all,' Madge said shakily. 'There's just one more thing, Seton. I'm resigning, as from *now*.' His brows came down like thunder, but she was already picking up her bag, and slinging her coat over her shoulder. 'I'm resigning from this job, from Studio Seven, and best of all,' she spat from the door, 'I'm resigning from *you*!'

Olivia Copleigh, her pale green dress perfectly matching the antiseptic décor of the ward, looked at her daughter with the cool green eyes known to every cinemagoer.

'You're not paying attention, Margot. Your father and I have something extremely important to tell you.'

'You and Daddy?' She looked abstractedly from her mother's face to her father's. Her father was looking much better tonight, his complexion almost ruddy, and much of his old debonair charm restored. 'I'm sorry,' she smiled tiredly. 'What is it?'

'We've been talking things over, Madgie,' her father said. 'Ever since I arrived in this country. We had a lot to say to each other. However, we wanted to wait until you were back from Tibet to tell you.'

'Tell me what?' Real curiosity made her forget Seton for a moment. 'What are you planning? Another film together?'

Her mother shook her head. 'Not for the time being.' She paused. 'Another marriage.'

Madge's mouth dropped open. Tyrone Copleigh looked across at his ex-wife with a smile, and reached out his hand. She took it between both of her own. Madge stared at the linked hands, unable to comprehend.

'Married?' she repeated. 'You two? Again?'

'It's not uncommon in the film world,' her father replied. 'Remember the Burtons?'

'Besides, someone has to keep your father in order,' her mother said tartly. But her mouth became tender as she looked across at him. 'And I seem to be the only one who knows how to do it.'

'We've been apart for too long,' he said, leaning back on the pillow and smiling at his daughter. 'Your mother and I were made for each other, Madgie. We should never have parted, all those years ago.' And with a rare moment of self-knowledge, added, 'God knows, we don't deserve to be inflicted on anyone else but each other!'

Madge sat transfixed.

'Now that all the storms are over,' her mother went on, 'there may be calm waters ahead for us both.'

'Calm at twilight,' her father nodded. 'God knows I've been a fool since the divorce—but all that's behind me now. We love each other, Madge. That's all there is to it—and now we're going to face our last years in harmony.'

'Together,' Olivia concluded. Her elegant brows peaked worriedly as she gazed at her daughter's open-mouthed face. 'Well, Margot?' she said with a touch of impatience, 'what do you think?'

Madge shut her mouth. For the second time that day emotions wrestled inside her madly. Disbelief, wry amusement, a hesitant joy, an insane desire to laugh, all struggled behind her wide eyes.

When she suddenly burst into tears, it was as much a surprise to Madge herself as to her astounded parents.

'My poor baby,' her father said, clambering out of bed to put his arm round her. 'Why, I never guessed it would mean this much to you.'

'Oh, it does,' she sobbed. 'I'm so delighted for you both.' She wiped the tears from her cheeks, and gave them a wobbly smile. 'Are you really serious about this?'

'Of course we're serious,' Olivia Copleigh said, raising her eyebrows. 'Why, we've got a major press-conference about it scheduled for tomorrow at ten . . .'

Madge didn't stay long afterwards, even though there were a thousand questions she wanted to ask them both. She was too tired, and her fight with Seton that morning had left her terribly drained and depressed. Besides, she knew that her parents would have much to say to each other now, many years to fill in.

The twilight was pale gold over the park, making the trees beautiful and mysterious, and reminding her of Lhasa. As she walked down the stairs to where her car was parked, Madge's feelings were oddly mixed. The world, it seemed, hadn't lost its ability to keep surprising her. Her parents, together again! Would it last? She couldn't say. Maybe, as her father had said, they deserved one another, and that was all. Perhaps they were that bit older and wiser; perhaps even, with the selfish pragmatism that had always been their strongest feature, coming together again was a kind of insurance. Insurance, that was, against the rapidly-approaching time when their looks and glamour would fade, and dazzled, youthful lovers would no longer be so readily found. The time when they would have little left except one another's tolerance.

Maybe when that time came they would even have more attention to spare for their daughter. With a flash of optimism, it occurred to Madge that this might mark the beginning of a real change in their disastrous family life. Maybe from here on they would all begin drawing closer to one another . . .

It was strange to be able to think about her parents so dispassionately. She had certainly grown more mature over the past few weeks! She got into her car, still feeling oddly mixed up. With all her heart she wanted their second marriage to succeed. And whatever happened, she would continue, as she had always done, to love them. Expecting nothing, demanding nothing, just constantly, helplessly loving.

I'm a loving machine, she thought sadly, starting the car. I can't help it. Just switch me on, and I never go off again . . .

The sun was down, and the summer evening was busy with roosting birds. Madge wasn't concentrating, and as she pulled out of her parking space she had to brake hard for the sleek Porsche that cut across her path, forcing her to stop. She knew who it was before he even got out of his car, and her heart was beating painfully fast as she switched off her engine and unfastened her seatbelt.

Seton pulled her door open and stared down at her with dark eyes.

'Are you ever going to be able to forgive me for the past eighteen months?' he asked quietly. With a little sob, Madge rose up to meet his embrace. He kissed her with a hunger that obliterated every other thought from her mind, his arms crushing her to him as though he meant never to let her go. For a long minute they clung together in the middle of the street, oblivious to the queue of cars which began to build up behind them. It was only when people began to sound their horns that he released her and smiled into her swimming eyes.

'It's taken me all afternoon to find you,' he said softly. 'Have you got a few minutes to spare for a cruel fool?'

'All the minutes in my life,' she said, joy making her lightheaded. The look in his eyes had told her, more than any words that could pass between them, that all waiting was over, that now there could be no more hesitancy or disguise between their hearts.

'Then wait for me while I get our cars out of the way.'

Madge stood on the sidewalk, her heart soaring, unaware of the curious faces in the impatiently-waiting cars. Seton pulled his Porsche across the street, and the waiting traffic surged past indifferently. She was filled with fierce pride as he walked across the street to her, so tall and masculine and beautiful. Her man, her love . . .

Seton took her face in his hands, and kissed her again, the restraint of months giving way to a passion that shook them both.

'My idol,' she laughed shakily as their lips parted. 'You've always been my idol, ever since I was a child.'

'I told you,' he said huskily, 'I don't collect hero-worshippers, Copleigh.' He pulled her close. 'But if you'll walk awhile, my sweet, I'll tell you what I want you to be.'

'I'm open to suggestions,' she smiled, the sharp pull of want for him almost a pain inside. Arms round each other, they walked down the stone steps into the park. The lake glinted silver among the friendly shadows of the trees. She rested her head against his shoulder, simply content to be lost in this bliss.

'My parents are getting married again,' she said dreamily.

'That sounds a wonderful idea,' he replied.

'Yes. Doesn't it . . .'

'Maybe marriages are back in vogue. Sweet Madge,' he said softly, 'I've been such a terrible coward about you!'

'Am I so frightening?' she teased, clinging to his arms as he turned to face her at the water's edge.

'Yes,' he nodded. 'You're real—and that's terrifying! You're gentle and kind, my darling one. And sexy, and brave, and clever.' His voice became rough. 'And so very beautiful.' This time he kissed her as tenderly as though her mouth were a fragrant rose, fragile and easily crushed. Their lips had a language of their own, caressing, tasting, exchanging the urgent sweetness of their desire . . .

'Being all those things,' she gasped softly as he released her, 'is at least preferable to having horns and scales—isn't it?'

'You could say that,' he smiled. 'But you terrified me right from the start, when you came up to me in the

corridor, your sweet face as open and as innocent as a
flower, and tried to tell me how much you admired my
work. I felt the power of what you did to me then—just
as I feel it now. It's something I have no control over,
Madge. I'm as helpless as the sea under the moon . . .'

'But why did you keep me so far away?' she sighed,
nestling into his arms. 'You were so cruel, and for so
long!'

'I know,' he groaned. 'I was so sure I was doing the
right thing in keeping my distance from you, so sure
that my love for you was something I had to fight,
stamp out. It's taken me until now to realise that I
might as well try and tear out my own heart! Oh,
Madge, will you ever be able to forgive me? I was fool
enough to think I could kill it, and keep myself safe in
the dark, sterile, loveless cell I'd built around myself.'

'This will never die,' she said blissfully, looking up
into the dark eyes that had haunted her dreams for so
long. 'This is for ever, my love.'

'It had better be,' he warned with a touch of his old
grimness. 'Wisdom may have come late—but I've
finally realised that I couldn't possibly live without you.
I warn you, Madge, I'm madly jealous of you.' He
looked at her wickedly. 'I went out and bought a bottle
of champagne when I heard that Charlie Molesworth
had jaundice.'

'Poor Charlie,' she gurgled, unable to stop her
laughter, 'he's just a good friend to me! Oh,' she added
softly, 'and thank you for getting him that Los Angeles
job—Signor Machiavelli.'

'Impudent hussy,' he said, sweeping her up in his
arms with bright eyes. She arched her neck in ecstasy as
he covered her face with kisses, his lips nuzzling her
ears, her throat, the sweet-scented hollow of her
collarbone, as though hungry for the taste of her skin.
Wanting him was a flame, a familiar fever in her blood.
'You once told me you felt like a cat,' he reminded her,

holding her close against his hard body, '—each time I touched you, you wanted to purr.'

'Mmm!'

'Well, my own reactions were rather more violent,' he growled, making her yelp softly as his sharp teeth took her lower lip in a rough caress. 'You wrecked all my carefully laid defences, Madge. For five years I'd been telling myself that love didn't exist; it took one look at your sweet face to prove me utterly, hopelessly wrong!' Her body was slim and fragrant in his arms, her uptilted breasts peaked against his chest. 'After Lana's death, I told myself that I was just going to have to do without love. That I wasn't fit to be responsible for any other human being's happiness. I built such a strong fortress around my heart. And you—you had to come along and blow the roof off, start challenging me to be a man again. Yes,' he nodded at her incredulous smile, 'that's what it amounted to. You gave me such wonderful dreams, Madge. Dreams that I could take care of you, give you the love I could see you hungering for, take responsibility for your innocent heart. You made me dream that I was capable of joy.' His voice became very soft. 'And better still, capable of giving joy. But the more you intoxicated me, the more I tried to fight down those feelings, tell myself it just wasn't possible, that it must all be just a delusion. I kept you at bay for eighteen months, my soul, trying to pretend you just didn't exist. But when Charlie went down a week before you were due to leave for Tibet, I simply couldn't hold back any longer.'

'You didn't exactly melt into my arms,' she reproached him, spreading her hands possessively across the span of his shoulders.

'Oh, I was still convinced I could keep you at arm's length,' he smiled. 'How very wrong I was! Right up until this afternoon I thought I could still keep you at arm's length. God, what a fool I was—when I think of how nearly I must have lost you, my blood runs cold!'

'You could never lose me,' she denied joyfully, 'I'll always be here! But—"right up until this afternoon"? What changed your mind today?'

'A particularly blinding flash of revelation,' he said with a wry shake of the head. 'Madge, all that stuff about wanting you to be my partner, go with me to the Arctic Circle—that was rubbish. Cowardly, fraudulent rubbish.'

'Funny,' she grinned, 'I've never associated you with cowardice and fraud.'

'Both were behind that invitation,' he sighed. 'I don't know how you resisted throwing your typewriter at my head. You see, I was terrified that you would leave the Studio—and me—for ever. I'd been desperately trying to find a way of keeping you close to me—yet I still didn't have the courage to admit the reason why! And all the time I was laying my little plans, I knew deep inside that it was all a front, that what I *really* wanted wasn't your work, but you—you as my wife, the most important person in my universe. Your heart, your soul, your maddeningly sweet body—for ever! The partnership, that trip to the North Pole—that was my mind's ridiculous way of disguising what my heart's been aching for these past months and more. Seeing you walk out today destroyed me, my love.' He laughed ruefully. 'I've never spent such a miserable damned day in my life—and by the time I'd recovered, and knew what I wanted to say to you, you'd disappeared!' He held her tight in his arms, his voice husky. 'Sweet Madge, tell me you can dismiss all the stupid things I said today as the ravings of a madman!'

'Does that mean I'm not going with you to the Arctic Circle?' she asked in tender mockery, not trusting herself to be serious yet. 'How very disappointing!'

'Dear fool, of course you're coming with me. You're

coming with me wherever I go in this wide world. But not just as my partner.'

'How, then?' she whispered dazedly.

'If you agree—as my true and honourable wife.'

There was no need for her to agree; Seton could see the tears in her eyes, and taste their salt on his tongue as he kissed them away.

'When I saw the Land Rover lying in the rubble on Kanchenjunga, I thought my heart had died inside me, Madge.' His face had suddenly become sombre, and she stroked his cheek with wondering fingers, still close to tears. 'If you'd been dead,' he said softly, 'I don't think I'd have come down off that mountain. There would have been nothing left of my life.'

'Don't talk like that,' she pleaded. 'I'm here, and I'm yours, darling—yours for as long as you want me.'

'That's for ever,' he smiled. His words were a warm caress against her parted lips. 'I love you, Madge. I've never been as close as this to another human being. Those nights in Tibet—ah, how I ached for you then! And I thought I was being so wise, so right, in holding back and treating you as though you didn't matter a damn—when all the time, I needed you as a drowning man needs air!'

'And I,' she whispered, shaken to her soul by the words, 'have always loved you. I can't remember a time when I didn't love you, Seton—and I can't imagine a time when I won't!'

'We've got so much time to make up,' he said, his voice husky against her lips. 'I don't know if we'll ever find days enough and years enough . . .'

'We'll try,' she promised, melting in the fire of his kiss.

'Yes,' he nodded, the sunset gilding the face that was a mask no longer, would never be a mask to her again, 'The future belongs to us, my love. As we belong to each other.'

'As I belong to you,' she whispered. 'As I always will.'

Take these 4 best-selling novels FREE

Yes! Four sophisticated, contemporary love stories by four world-famous authors of romance FREE, as your introduction to the Harlequin Presents subscription plan. Thrill to **Anne Mather**'s passionate story BORN OUT OF LOVE, set in the Caribbean.... Travel to darkest Africa in **Violet Winspear**'s TIME OF THE TEMPTRESS....Let **Charlotte Lamb** take you to the fascinating world of London's Fleet Street in MAN'S WORLD .... Discover beautiful Greece in **Sally Wentworth**'s moving romance SAY HELLO TO YESTERDAY.

Harlequin Presents...

The very finest in romance fiction

Join the millions of avid Harlequin readers all over the world who delight in the magic of a really exciting novel. EIGHT great NEW titles published EACH MONTH! Each month you will get to know exciting, interesting, true-to-life people .... You'll be swept to distant lands you've dreamed of visiting .... Intrigue, adventure, romance, and the destiny of many lives will thrill you through each Harlequin Presents novel.

Get all the latest books before they're sold out!
As a Harlequin subscriber you actually receive your personal copies of the latest Presents novels immediately after they come off the press, so you're sure of getting all 8 each month.

Cancel your subscription whenever you wish!
You don't have to buy any minimum number of books. Whenever you decide to stop your subscription just let us know and we'll cancel all further shipments